# Black Curio

(a collection of short stories by Jon Goode)

Printed in the United States of America

First Printing, 2024

ISBN: 978-0-9965004-3-2

GOODESTUFF ENT LLC

Cover Art: Dr. Fahamu Pecou

Graphic Design: Verbal Slick

Editor: Dr. Lia T. Bascomb

Editor: Katina Pappas-DeLuca

Dedicated

to **John E Goode Jr.**

the best storyteller I've ever known,

and to **Joshua Goode**

the next chapter in the story.


Other Books by Jon Goode:

**Conduit: A Collection of Short Stories**

**Mydas: A Novel**


About the Author:

Jon Goode is an Emmy nominated writer raised in Richmond, VA and currently residing in Atlanta, GA. Jon's work has been featured in CNN's Black in America, HBO's Def Poetry Jam, BET's Lyric Café and TVOne's Verses and Flow. He has also written radio commercials for McDonalds, print ads for Nike, and written and appeared in commercials, vignettes and interstitials for MTV, Comedy Central, VH-1 and TVLand/ Nick@Nite. Jon's work earned him the 2006 Promax Gold for the best copyright in North America. In 2022 he won a gold American Advertising Award for Branded Content and Entertainment Non-Broadcast, a Silver Telly Award, and was again nominated for a Promax. Jon's collection of poems and short stories, Conduit, was #1 on Amazon for sixteen weeks. His debut novel, Mydas, was a #1 new title on Amazon for five weeks. Jon is a Fellow of AIR Serenbe, and a host and storyteller with The Moth.

# Preface

In the summer of 2023 I was working on a novel entitled, *The King Stays on the Board*, when I was invited by George Dawes Green and the non-profit organization 100 Miles to come down to St. Simons Island to collaborate on a storytelling project. St Simons is a beautiful island on the Georgia coast. I accepted the invitation because as a rule I don't turn down invitations to beautiful islands. One morning we drove over to Valona, a small tight-knit community right on the water, to interview a woman (Captain Cindy) that had transformed an aging shrimping boat into a successful coastal touring boat. The interview went swimmingly well and afterwards, as I was walking along the dock, I spotted in the distance a ceramic figurine sitting on a ladder facing the water. As I got closer I noticed it was an old, weathered, pickaninny figurine (pickaninny figurines, or dolls, are racist caricatures of Black children that came to prominence in the 1930s). Initially I thought, "Run!" but I didn't. Instead I did the thing we tell people in horror movies not to do, I walked closer and closer until it was right in front of me. The figurine sat perched, outfitted in a paint chipped white shirt with rolled up sleeves and tan overalls, staring out at the serene coastal waters as they lapped gently against the shore. The doll appeared to be reminiscing, or maybe meditating, or possibly plotting. Whatever it was or wasn't doing no one else seemed to be aware of its existence. It was as if I was the only person in the world (or at least in Valona) that could see it. I stared at the figurine and began imagining what it was thinking. Wondering how long it had been there. Envisioning the life it had lived, the people it had seen, and the people that hadn't seen it. I drove back to the home I was staying in on St. Simons Island and began writing the short story "The Curio Case of Benson Stone."

After I was done writing "The Curio Case" I dropped it into a folder on my computer labeled, short stories. I realized I had quite a few stories in that folder. Some I'd actually forgotten I'd even written. I began re-reading them all and realized I had enough stories that I really really liked to begin thinking about collecting them into a volume. So, I grabbed some tales I'd written based on my experiences on the 89 MARTA bus, a few prequel stories I'd written just for myself to serve as a foundation for *The King Stays on the Board*, two short film scripts, and some stand-alone narratives. I searched for the through lines in each, and then used the story "The Curio Case," as an anchor to pull them all together into *Black Curio*.

*Black Curio* is a collection of stories that live in the now, the not-so-distant past, and the far-flung future of the Black experience. There are true stories from private spaces and public transit, almost true stories from office buildings and chess parks, and imagined realities from worlds not yet born. There are moments of tears, smiles, and laughter that I hope will resonate with you the reader and give you cause to sit, examine, and reflect. I hope and pray you enjoy reading them as much as I enjoyed writing them. Thank you for your support. I never take it for granted. Cheers!

# Table of Contents:

1. The Boy With Fire In His Heart || a Fable                                    4

2. Essentially || a Tale from the 89 || Fiction                                9

3. That Masked Man || a Tale from the 89 || True                              40

4. Change Gone Come || a Tale from the 89 || True-ish                         47

5. Buttermilk || Historical Fiction                                          53

6. Pluto || The King Stays on the Board || True-ish                          66

7. Obama Phone || The King Stays on the Board || Fiction                     71

8. Mourning Joe || The King Stays on the Board || True-Enough                81

9. Six Minutes || a Club Quarantine Story || Fiction                         94

10. Blacc Koffee: A Pop-Up || Fiction                                       121

11. Yellovely || Fiction                                                    147

12. The Curio Case of Benson Stone || Fiction                               163

13. Bolie || Fiction                                                        223

14. Rose Colored Glasses || Short Screenplay                                237

15. Prestidigitation || Short Screenplay                                    251

16. The King Stays on the Board || Novel || First Chapter preview           270

# *The Boy with Fire in His Heart*

[a Fable]

# The Boy with Fire in His Heart
## [a Fable]

Once upon a distant lifetime, and thrice upon a future lifeline, in a village just north of known space and just beyond recorded life's time, on the edge of light and dark there once was a boy with fire in his heart.

Legends relay that villagers say, they remember that when he was born in his heart there was just an ember. Something they deemed of no harm. Something that once seen they planned to use to keep the village warm.

An ember in one's heart was not the norm, and though they didn't understand it they counted it a blessing to behold. A possible source of warmth when life turned impossible and cold. A possible source of light on dark nights when monsters beneath beds grew irrational and bold.

Legends relay that villagers say, that as the boy grew the ember grew too right before their eyes' sight. What was really true was that it didn't really grow as he grew in height, but grew as he grew in the understanding of the purpose of his life.

You see, for eons many in the village went along to get along. Sour notes had stolen their sweet songs as the world's burdens rested on their weak, weary, thin arms and shoulders. They lived a life of hand to mouth as they grew weak, weary, thin, and older. They lived a life full of doubt, and each week their hearts grew clearly colder and colder. They mindlessly worked, nose to the cornmeal stone. They tirelessly worked

5

their hands and heels to the bone. Their eyes, blurry, always on the ground, on their bruises, on their scars. While this boy with a growing ember in his heart had his eyes in the clouds, and amongst the stars.

One day while standing by the ulimwengu bush, the bush that all in the village looked to for sustenance and health, the boy stared into the sky and the stars and saw two things; the faces of the gods, and himself. The ember began to pound and ignite in his chest. It kindled everything to his right and his left. It went from flickering and tame, to a quickly growing flame, to an uncontrollable blaze. The villagers were amazed and frightened all the same at the sight of this first spark. Something that had been little more than a coal in a warm hearth, now seemed like a fire large enough to consume a whole house. Someone pointed and gave a scream, a warning, a shout, "In our village lives a boy with a fire in his heart!"

The heat from his heart burned down the ulimwengu bush, its fruit, leaves, and roots. The fire consumed the only way the villagers believed they knew to meet their needs, and grow food. There were those in the village that screamed, indeed the boy would need to leave soon. Sadness broke the levee behind the boy's eyes like a monsoon, and tears began to stream. Those tears mixed with the ash from the ulimwengu bush and some ancient forgotten seeds. The boy's sad cries and screams created a mighty breeze, and slowly people began to point and look. The earth gently shook and growing where once stood the ulimwengu bush were long lost mbinguni trees. Trees that would produce enough fruit to forever meet all of the village's wants and needs. A blessing indeed.

The boy was allowed to stay, and all the night and half the day he would stare at the sky and the stars, and there see himself and the face of the gods. All the while the fire in his heart burnt steadily. Then one day he saw not only himself and the gods, but his destiny. Everything he was destined to be. In his excitement he couldn't hold it, the fire in his chest exploded. Again the villagers screamed their angry remarks, "In our village lives a boy with a fire in his heart!"

The vibration from his heart's exploding sound knocked the old damn down. The lowlands were flooded now. The villager's voices began to resound that this wasn't what they would want nor what they would need. They were thankful for the mbinguni trees but again felt the boy would soon need to leave. This time he stood still as a tomb in his knowledge of himself, and the destiny he'd seen. Then the water receded and vines proceeded to grow and intertwine with robust grapes in-between. To a land that had for ages stood barren and anemic the grapes brought wages and wealth unseen. The villagers made sweet wine, and wrapped herbs, rice and meat in the grape leaves. They had a feast that few could believe. A blessing indeed.

The boy was again allowed to stay, and again all the night and half the day he would stare at the sky and the stars, where he would see himself, his destiny, and the face of the gods. And the fire in his heart burnt steadily. Then one day he saw not only himself, the face of the gods, and his destiny, but the destiny of the village too. His heart and the fire grew. The villagers gathered around, they realized that the fire in one's heart is not something to run from but something to run to.

As the flame began to jump, spit, and spark, with great pride and joy every man, woman, girl, and boy began to remark, sing, and shout to the top of the mbinguni trees, "In our village lives a boy with a fire in his heart! And he is a blessing indeed!"

And if you ever need something to believe in ...

Remember once upon a distant lifetime, and thrice upon a future lifeline, in a village just north of known space and just beyond recorded life's time, on the edge of light and dark there once was a boy with fire in his heart...

and his heart is still beating.

At least that's what legends relay, and villagers say,

and I, indeed, believe them.

# *Essentially*

[a Tale from the 89 || Fiction]

## ***Essentially***
## [a Tale from the 89 || Fiction]

You're damn right I'm an essential worker! It just took a global pandemic for someone to say it out loud, that's all. Who am I? you ask. Shit, who are you?

Okay, okay I'll tell you who I am. I'll go first. I drive the number eighty-nine up and down Ol' Nat'al Highway. Some people say, Old National Highway. They probably also pronounce both T's in Atlanta, which they shouldn't. I'm sure they enunciate the words, Old National, with great clarity. Say them in such a way that their lips go into a pucker and then pull back showing all of their teeth. We call people who pucker and then teeth, tourists. When you say it right, like a native ATLien from the soufside, your mouth lives somewhere between a smile and a sneer. Which happens to be exactly where Ol' Nat resides as well.

Yes, I drive the eighty-nine through rain, sleet, and please God don't let it snow. The eighty-nine is a carriage, a modern day stagecoach if you will, that shuttles people to their daily obligations where money is made. It ushers groups to after dark activities where money is spent, and takes individuals any and everywhere in-between. Riding the eighty-nine is heaven on an eighty degree day with the windows down and the city spilling all its secrets. It's a perpetual purgatory for some, a weigh station with Thoth's finger heavy on the scale. It can be hell on the first and fifteenth when them checks hit and the narcotic escapism of choice flows freely. On the eighty-nine I've seen people break up and make up. I've seen people get their life, and almost lose it. I've watched folk find religion, and lose their lunch. For some it's the only quiet moment in their day. For others it's the only place where they feel safe. Whatever it is to you, it'll be that for a thirty to forty five minute bumpy, stop and go, slice of life.

Listen, the eighty-nine is essential and I drive it. So what does that make me? And who are you again?

Anyway, I was on the bus reading the AJC early one morning before I started my route. This was about three months ago, before the pandemic. You know, back before people started slamming their elbows into yours just to say hello, and collecting toilet paper like it was a Pokémon. I was flipping to the sports section so I could see just how badly my Falcons had gotten beaten. Look, I'm not saying their defeat was a given. I'm just saying after Super Bowl LI my faith, and their play, hadn't been the best. Well, on this particularly warm fall morning, with the red of the sunrise receding back into the horizon, and the humidity still as thick a Popeye's biscuits, this dude they call Leg-Bruh boarded at the stop near the trees at Old Nat and Burdett. He's a rare cat. Dude is always singing this song no one seems to know, or can even hear. On that morning he boarded and jokingly said to anyone that would listen,

"A boy stood before a judge after being viciously beaten by both parents. When asked by the magistrate who he wanted to live with he said, the Atlanta Falcons! The judge said, why the Falcons!? The boy said, because the Falcons don't viciously beat nobody!"

Leg-Bruh laughed. The whole bus laughed with him. My Falcons gambling losses wouldn't allow me to find the humor in it. Anyway, I was looking at the paper when I came across an article that read,

*With the rise in Uber, Lyft and those damn suicide scooters that people just throw anywhere   like a five year old with Cheerios,*

maybe it didn't say the Cheerios part,

*with their rise does Atlanta even need MARTA anymore.*

Does Atlanta need MARTA!? Does the Pope need that pointy hat!? Well, maybe not but he's better with it ain't he?

For those of you unfamiliar, MARTA is Atlanta's transit authority. The buses and trains that keep the city moving for two dollars and fifty cent a pop, that's MARTA. It stands for Metro Atlanta Rapid Transit Authority. Some people like to say it stands for Moving Africans Rapidly Through Atlanta. We call those people, Republicans. They are the same people that oppose MARTA expansion because they say it'll bring crime to their neighborhoods. Because that's what people do, steal your big screen TV and take it with them on the damn bus.

Anyway, all of that is beside the point, what I'm trying to say is, MARTA is essential in these days and times because that rideshare shit ain't cheap! It's at least five dollars to go three blocks. THREE BLOCKS! You're thinking why don't people just walk the three blocks. Well for one, Mrs. Mabel got the asthma, the gout, and the sugars. She's barely walking three yards, and she's not alone. For two, those boys with the sagging pants can't safely walk one block with their trousers down around their thighs. They'll get a rash, look like a pox, trying to walk three blocks in that state. And yeah sure, folk could suicide scooter three blocks, but people's balance and attention span ain't what it used to be. I think it's the tennis shoes that look like a Transformer, and not being able to go a minute without looking at their phones.

I once saw a guy with a face full of tattoos, and wearing some skinny saggy jeans. Don't ask me how they were skinny and saggy. He had on a hat that read, *Fck Ur Feelins*, and a hoodie that read, *God is Dope*. He, and the messaging in his clothes, were all over the place. He was near Jerome Road clearly trying to commit seppuku via scooter while taking a picture of himself with his Y phone. He had one hand on the handlebars and the other holding his phone high in the air so that he could get a good angle of all those tattoos. That's when he lost balance, almost sideswiped a pole, jumped the curb into oncoming traffic, miraculously scooted across four lanes like Jesus walking-it-out on the sea of Galilee, hit the curb on the other side and flew off like Jazzy Jeff getting thrown outta Uncle Phil's house. He skinned his forehead to the white meat right in front of Big Daddy's Soul Food joint! He rubbed all the tattoos right off his forehead. I'm talking about several hundred dollars of ink asphalt-dry-erased off his face. I stopped the bus, opened the door, and yelled for him to put some Vicks salve on it, and pull up his pants next time. Would pulling up his pants have saved his forehead? Probably not, but he's better with 'em up ain't he?

Anyway, what I'm trying to say is you can go three blocks in a rideshare for five dollars, or you can ride across town, and watch a live tattoo removal on MARTA for two dollars and fifty cent. It's an entertainment bargain! It's live-action real-life Tubi.

Plus here's the further truth of it, people working two and three jobs and still barely making ends meet depend on MARTA. People who keep their too warm, and slightly damp, money in their bra, and bank at those check cashing spots that also sell lace fronts and chicken wings, rely on MARTA. Folk who only have the twenty minutes from the time they get on the bus, until the time they get off the bus, to get the only sound sleep they're going to get all day need MARTA. Don't let the movie studios, fake housewife tv shows, and mumbling rappers fool you. Atlanta has more people like those that take the MARTA than those that don't. So when they instituted the COVID lockdown and said only essential personnel were to report to work, guess who showed up? Me.

Yeah, the world came off the tracks a few months and weeks back. People call it COVID or the Pandemic but it's government name, what its mama calls it, is Coronavirus. When I first heard the name I thought it just meant a person with a drinking problem. I wanted to tell 'em having a Corona virus ain't nothing. I know people with the Schlitz Malt Liquor virus. Now that's a killer. I soon found out, this wasn't about falling off the wagon, this was about staying on the planet. Things got serious fast. The president—you know the one, the fake billionaire with the fake hair—he said, it's all under control and we have nothing to worry about. He also said, inject yourself with bleach and shine a UV light up your ass. That's when I knew we were in trouble. I ain't never seen anyone that calls shit sugar like that dude. If he called today and told me I'd live forever, I'd know for sure I'm dying tomorrow.

Anyway, the next thing you know everyone was told to stay at home, wash their hands while singing "Whistle While You Twurk," and practice social distancing. Old people started getting sick like you wouldn't believe. Young people started going to the beach like you wouldn't believe. Hospitals became overwhelmed. People started to die. Curfews were established and the word came down. Only essential personnel were to report to work.

Some of the people they all of sudden started considering essential, like grocery store clerks, food workers, and liquor store cashiers didn't have cars. Many of the people headed to grocery stores, liquor stores, their weed man, and other essential places of business didn't have cars either. They take the buses and trains. So suddenly in a way that has never been voiced before, WE, the workers many people ignore, that have the jobs that most consider dead-end, became essential. So every day I get up out of my warm bed, while my even warmer wife is still asleep, and I get people to where they need to be, up and down Ol' Nat'al Highway.

The nation doesn't have enough gloves and masks for the hospital workers so you know they don't have enough for bus drivers. When I asked my supervisor about safety gear he told me to stay behind the plexiglass shield that separates the drivers from the riders, and to try not to breath so much. So I head to work these days wearing a pair of the bright yellow plastic gloves my wife uses to clean the toilet, and a mask she made by cutting one of her bras in half. I think she learned that on Youtube. I don't mind it being pink but the lace is a bit much. She asked me how it fit and I told her, it fits pretty good but it smells like a cell phone, a pack of cigarettes, and fifteen too-warm-damp-dollars. She laughed and said, well that's good because the other one smells like a debit card, half a blunt, and Ramen Noodles. The Ramen Noodles is egregious. As I leave every morning I tell her I'll keep her abreast of my day. She loves me, but she hates my puns. I refuse to go tit for tat with her.

Anyway, today I hop on the bus at 6 a.m. and wipe it down. I use Clorox wipes on the steering wheel, the seat, and the panel. I have a thing of wipes sitting out so that anyone that boards can do the same. I get off the bus, walk its perimeter, and do an inspection. I look at the tires. I look at the body, and dammit man! Someone has spray painted, MARTA 89, on the side of the bus and then lined through MARTA and written COVID above it, and lined through the 8 and written a 1. So now it reads, COVID 19. Is nothing sacred!? Some people already think of the buses and trains as moving virus factories. Now this. There's nothing I can do about it at the moment. I need to start my route. I adjust the driver's seat, sit down, fire her up and pull out.

Ridership is down, way down, there is no denying that. People are scared and with good reason. The number of people catching the virus is alarming. The number of people dying is growing fast. Times are hard, and money is tight. I was told by my boss to not deny anyone a ride. If they can pay, good. If they can't, no worries, get on the bus. Very few people board on my first two trips up and down. A lady trying to get to The Dollar General the second it opens. An old man that looks like he used to box, but he says it's the wrong bus. A young man that runs on, scrambles to the back, and ducks down for three lights before raising his head and looking out of the windows to see if anyone is following him. A young lady with three small children headed south down Old Nat. The kid's all look at my pink, lace, bra-mask and laugh. The youngest, not quite one, starts pulling at his mom's shirt to feed. The trips are fairly uneventful until the 8:45 a.m. stop at the corner of Bethsaida and Old Nat.

I pass the Shell gas station just before Bethsaida and I see him standing up at the next stop. Morris. I ask myself, can I just act like I didn't see him and let the next bus pick him up? He's got a sign in one hand, and his other is buried down the front of his pants. Purell could never, in all its glory, sanitize that hand. Morris liberates his hand from his pants and begins waving it wildly to get my attention. Shit, now I done looked at him. Now I've got to stop. I pull the bus over. He puts his hand back down the front of his pants, and boards the bus slowly dragging a sign behind him. He stares at me, and smiles like a man walking into Magic City for the first time. I don't say anything. I look straight ahead.

He starts,

"Good morning, Virgil. **Big facts**!"

The *Big facts* exclamation is a Tourettes like tick. Morris usually makes a statement and follows it with some kind of random, loud, interjection.

I return his greeting, politely, like my mama taught me to do,

"Good morning, Morris."

Morris is a gentle, but slightly annoying, homeless soul. He panhandles to get food, shelter, and bus fare. He generally spouts, without provocation or ceasing, his theories about how people are now made of impossible-beyond meat, how there's a pirate ship buried beneath Vine City, and how avocados are really unhatched dragon eggs.

"I don't have the fare. **Not fair**!" Morris says.

I tell him, it's fine. Get on the bus. He boards and stands near the front. Near me. His smile widens and he says,

"I told you, didn't I? **Trick get off me**!"

He points to his sign. The sign itself is just a piece of square, brown, cardboard. The piece of cardboard, however, is affixed to a baseball bat. Written on the sign, in black magic marker, are the words, "I told you didn't I!" minus the, trick get off me.

He continues,

"I told everyone this was going to happen. **Das Efx**! That a virus was coming and it would shut down the whole world. **In his hands**! But noooo it was Morris is homeless. Morris is crazy. Morris talks to dead people! **Bruce Willis**! But Morris was right wasn't he! Wasn't I Virgil! **Trick get off me**!"

I'm starting to think the, *trick get off me*, is less of a tick and more of a pointed attack. I take a deep breath, the breath my supervisor told me not to take, and say,

"Yes, Morris. You've been saying that for years."

"That's right! And you know what else, I know who done it. I know who unleashed the 'Rona on us and it won't no damn bats!" He shakes the baseball bat like Babe Ruth calling his shot.

18

"Bats are the scapegoat, or scapebat. **Batman**! You want to know who did it? **Who's Johnny she said**!"

"I don't," I whisper.

Morris slides a little closer and whispers back,

"Well, Morris is going to tell you anyway," and then yells, "Morris is going to tell you all!"

He turns toward the rest of the bus with an excitement that turns to disappointment when he discovers the bus is empty. Everyone has gotten off within the last three stops. He shrugs, turns back to me and says,

"Well, Morris is going to tell you. **Just meeeee and youuuu**!"

He leans over as close to the plexiglass shield as he can get. His breath fogs against the clear acrylic. I have never been so happy to have a plexiglass shield in my life. He says, with heavy breath and through teeth spaced out like a picket fence,

"It was the poo dogs, Virgil. The Poo dogs! **Atomic Dog**!"

"The poo dogs?" I ask before I can catch myself.

"Yes sir! The Yorkiepoo, the Morkiepoo, the Shih-poo! **Snoop Doggy Dogg**!"

Jesus Christ and all the saints, he done blamed a global pandemic on Ol' Nat Yeller.

Morris has been wrestling with his mind for some time. The thing is he wasn't always this way. I know his people, his folk, his mama dem. His dad, Big Morris, drove greyhound buses with my dad. I can still see

19

my dad in his light grey uniform headed off to work in the wee hours of the morning. So early God was still yawning. I'd be up eating Cream of Wheat because my mom said it would stick to my ribs. Who wants sticky ribs? Anyway, I hated Cream of Wheat but I loved my dad. I was so proud, you know. I'd tell anyone that would listen that my dad drove the big buses. He wanted so much for me, and I just wanted to be just like him. Turns out I did. He passed when both he and I were young. He lived loud but not long. Who knows, maybe that's the best way. But sometimes when I get on the bus in the morning, and even during the day while I'm driving, I imagine him standing, right where Morris is now, and looking at me with the same pride in his eyes that I had when I used to look at him. Yeah.

As for Morris's mother, Mrs. Margaret was a school teacher. She taught me fifth grade. I almost failed fifth grade. I couldn't make two and two equal four, for nothing. She'd say what's two and two and I'd reply, Tutu? She was a nice lady but either you did the work and passed the tests, or you lived to see her for another year. I just barely escaped being in the fifth grade for the tutu'd time.

I would say that between his mother and his father Morris was destined to be relatively bright. Turns out he wasn't relatively bright, he was a genius. I remember when he was a young Eggbert outsmarting every Foghorn Leghorn in the neighborhood. He was definitely the smartest person I'd ever met. He finished high school at fifteen. He finished Harvard by eighteen and was doing some Pinky and the Brain shit at MIT for the government by twenty-two. Yeah, he was in Cambridge trying to figure out how to put toothpaste back in the tube, or some other equally impossible thing. But the mind, I hear, can be like a rubber band. You can only stretch it so far before it snaps. Once it snaps, well, it ain't a rubber band no more.

Anyway, way before the world got drunk on Corona and ordinary people like myself got called essential, Morris was already considered such by the government. Here's the thing about the government and essential personnel though, once you're no longer essential to them you no longer exist. Once his rubber band of a brain snapped they sent Morris back to Atlanta with a thank you, a fresh pocket protector, and a fist full of anti-psychotic meds. Ever since, he plays chess in the park, lives beneath an overpass, talks to dead people, and uses a black magic marker to write signs telling everyone, I told you so.

So when he says, Lassie-poo sicked a virus on the planet, I can't begrudge him that. I just look straight ahead and keep driving. I can see out of my periphery that he's just standing there staring at me like Jack Nicholson with his head through a freshly splintered door panel. So I say,

"Dogs huh?"

"Yes, the dogs! Have you noticed that dogs can't get the virus? **Hot dog**! They're immune!"

I say, "I did hear something about that on CNN."

"Don't listen to CNN, Fox, MSNBC, any of them! The dogs had them spayed and neutered! **Allergic to nuts**!"

"You really think it's the dogs don't you Morris?"

"I do and I'm dog gone right," he points to his, "I told you didn't I," sign. He continues, his energy rising,

"And it's not the German Shepherds, Pit bulls, Rottweilers, Doberman's, no not those dogs. They just want to shit in your shoe and hump your leg when you got company over. **Bump and Grind**! No, it's the Frankenstein dogs! The poo dogs!"

"The poo dogs huh?"

"And the Morkies!"

"The Morkies?"

"Yes! The Morkies are the masterminds! **Thinking of a master plan**! Who else could have pinned it on the bats? But that's what the bats get for pinning swine flu on the pigs. But then again the pigs pinned avian flu on the birds. **Morris Day**!"

"Morris, my wife and I have a Morkie. We named her Morkie Mindy. Nanu Nanu."

"Abandon all of your possessions and move out of that house immediately. Your life and your wife's life are in danger Virgil! They look cute but they're little furry balls of death! **Big balls!**"

I think back on the number of times I've almost tripped over that dog and fallen down the steps to my death. Why the hell is Morkie Mindy always by the staircase when I'm trying to go down the steps? I don't see that dog any other hour of the day except when she's trying to Jack and Jill me. And why the hell am I now entertaining Morris's poo brained theories? Sweet fancy Moses! I'm gone have to get my own

22

rubber band checked!.

"And you know what else Virgil!?"

"No, I don't know what else, and I don't think I want to know what else! You already got me ready to call Mike Vick to come get my dog!"

"Well, Morris will tell you anyway. They also put COVID-19 in the icing of Krispy Kreme donuts but it's only active when the hot and ready light is on. **Just give me the light**!"

"God damn you Morris! Now you've gone too far! You take that back. You've attacked a sacred cow now Morris! You can slander my dog, you could have even talked trash about my titty-mask if you wanted too, but don't you ever attack the goodness that is Krispy Kreme! When my Lord calls me home, if there is a light at the end of the tunnel, I pray it reads hot and ready!"

Before I can espouse the further virtues of Krispy Kreme I catch the silhouette of someone standing up at the next bus stop. Oh, I'd know that silhouette anywhere. Where Morris was a stop I had considered skipping, this is one I never skip. Miss Alexus.

I pull the bus over and happily swing the door open. Morris puts his hand back inside his pants, and begins to exit as Alexus boards.

"This is my stop Virgil! My mom told me you almost failed K5. Don't let yourself be killed by K-9! **Trick get off me**!"

More and more I see why my wife doesn't care for puns. Morris rushes down the steps past Alexus. Alexus's face is twisted in anger and confusion.

"Why is his hand in his pants? And did he just call me a trick!?" she says, spinning around ready to confront Morris.

"No no no! He was calling me a trick. I mean he wasn't calling anyone a trick. I mean he was but his rubber band is messed up."

I sigh because I know none of that makes any sense. I look over and Morris is at the foot of the steps openly staring at Alexus his mouth agape. She still has on the five inch glass heels common to her profession. Attached to the shoes are satin straps that wrap around legs that seem to be as long as the beanstalk Jack climbed, and look to be strong enough to drop kick the giant at the top. Alexus wears a white thin jacket with her name bedazzled on the back in rhinestones. The faux gems catch the light with her every step. The jacket hangs just a bit longer than her short shorts. This gives the impression that she's not wearing any pants at all. She's mocha complected but uses makeup to lighten her appearance. Her neck still tells the truth of it. Her eyelashes bat like fly swatters at a June picnic in Macon. Her shoulder length hair is parted down the middle and frames her round eyes, painted cheekbones, and red red lips. In the south, pretty and fine are not the same thing. A woman with a beautiful face is considered pretty. A woman with a killer shape is considered fine. Alexus is pretty and fine.

I see Morris still standing at the foot of the steps, staring at exactly what I'm staring at. Alexus looks ready to charge back down the steps and let Morris know who is what, when I say,

"What are you looking at Morris!"

"I'm crazy Virgil. Not blind. Also your dad said, there was always oatmeal if you didn't want to eat the cream of wheat. **Choices**!"

My dad? I'm completely caught off guard by this.

"What? When … Morris, when did he say that to you?"

"When I got on the bus he was standing right where I was standing. Right there. **Be right there!**"

Morris points to the floor of the bus. To a space beside and slightly behind the plexiglass. Right where he'd been standing,

"Alright Virgil! **Swayze**!"    With that Morris walks off. His feet moving swiftly one behind the other in short choppy steps. His sign and head are held high. I close the door and look to where Morris pointed. Alexus walks up and, unknowingly, stands in that exact spot. She reaches into a backpack and pulls out a purse that would need a purse to carry anything. She begins searching through it. It's not a long search.

"I can't find my MARTA card, Virgil"

I keep staring at the spot on the floor. It's as if she isn't there.

She says,

"Virgil? You okay?"

I pull myself back into the now,

"Yes. Yes, I'm okay, and it's okay," I say as I close the door and pull off.

"Well thank you Virgil," she says as she works to keep her balance on the rocking bus.

Just as she turns to find a seat I ask a question,

"People still coming to the strip club, Miss Alexus?"

She stops, turns back to me, squints her eyes and says,

"Adult entertainment venue, Virgil."

"True, true, true. People still coming to the adult entertainment venue? With this virus thing going on?"

"Of course they are. When have men let a little thing like death keep them from staring at a shaking ass?"

Alexus throws her head back and laughs. I move to my next question.

"True, true, true. What about you? How does it work for you and the girls?"

She squints her eyes and says,

"Women, Virgil. We aren't girls."

"True, true, true."

She takes a deep breath, rolls her eyes, and says,

"Well the first thing I do is put on my mask," she raises her right hand and around her wrist is a white mask that has clearly been bedazzled by whoever did her jacket. She continues,

"Well, you know what, that's actually the second thing I do. The first thing I do is change into my costume, do my stretches, and warm up by making my ass clap loud enough to turn off all the lights in an old folks home."

I squint my eyes and say,

"Adult retirement community."

She pauses for a second and then laughs.

"True, true, true. Well, after that I put on my mask. Where'd you get your mask Virgil? That's a cute mask. The color. The lace. Strawn-jay! So, after making my ass clap louder than Thanos snapping his fingers, and putting on my mask I..."

I continue up Old Nat. Alexus continues speaking about masks, adult entertainment venue safety protocols, and gluteus produced rounds of applause. She's passionate about her work. Usually I'd be passionate about the details of her work. Today, however, my mind returns to what Morris just said. How could Morris have known about the Cream of Wheat? I mean he's smart but is he, Miss Cleo with a 1-800 number-a Ja-faking accent-and a crystal ball-smart?

I look down at Alexus's feet. She's still stands where Morris was standing. Where Morris said my dad was, is, standing? Jesus is she standing on him with those clear heeled shoes? I bet they could hurt the dead. Is she standing inside him? Is he getting some sort of otherworldly lap dance as we speak? Talk about raising the dead. Oh, my mom would not like that at all. No. She'd kill herself just so she could go to heaven and slap his face.

Anyway, there have been many days where it's felt like he's still with me. You know? Looking over me. There was this day, a couple of weeks back, when I was looking for my keys in the basket by the door. That's where they always are. On this day, they weren't there and I couldn't find them. I literally turned the basket upside down and right side up. No keys. Then ten minutes later, there they were, right there in the basket. I left the house, turned on the radio, and heard about a bad accident. A hit and run that involved what was described as a yellow-ish car with a vanity plate. It happened along what would have been my route to work, ten minutes prior. It sent a shiver down my spine because, well, because even though I acted like I didn't know, I did. Life is not all good luck, and coincidence, and knock on wood. There's been someone, my dad, looking out for me. Has been since the day I was born. Will be until the day I die. And, God willing, I'll do the same for my son. I don't think I've ever let myself really think that thought. I don't think I ever imagined it would feel so good to do so.

I never really said the things I wanted to say to my dad. I don't know why. Maybe pride. Dumb male macho shit. Whatever. Anyway, I never really told him how much I loved him. How proud I felt of him every day of my life. What I feel to be true is that he's right here, right now, and so I just say it. I turn to where Alexus is standing and say,

"I'm proud of you. I always have been. I'm sorry I didn't say it sooner."

I'm not really looking at Alexus. I'm looking past her, through her, to wherever in the ether my dad is standing. Oh, but Alexus is looking at me. Alexus is looking at me like she looked at Morris when she thought he'd called her a trick. I go to explain myself but before I can she dissolves into tears.

"I don't know why you said that Virgil but thank you. Jesus. I think I've been waiting for someone to say that to me my whole life, I just didn't know it. I read a quote the other night, 'There is a crack, a crack in everything. That's how the light gets in.' It was written on Brandy's ass near her ass crack so I don't know what that means to her but to me it spoke to the unhealed hurt I've experienced with my family. But it's through the wound of that same hurt that your words have touched me. Jesus Virgil. My God, what made you say that?"

I pause for a second or two. Not entirely sure of what to say next. So, I just tell her the truth.

"I thought you might be standing in the spirit of my father."

She stares at me for a moment. Then she says,

"Amen," and begins to clap but I don't see her hands moving.

She continues,

"Amen Virgil! We are all standing in the spirit of the father aren't we."

I try to interject and let her know that I'm being literal. Let her know that her clear heels are probably front and center inside the spiritual projection of my deceased papa, but she will hear none of it.

Then she says,

"Virgil. Do you like me?"

What in the hell! Listen, a man's eyes would have to be in his foot not to see that Alexus is an attractive woman. And who doesn't like that? Oh, but one thing Atlanta will certainly teach you is that everything that looks good ain't good for you plus I'm a mainly happily married man. So that's what I stutter, and say to her, leaving out the mainly part.

"Alexus, I'm a happily married man."

"You can be happily married and still like me. Two things can be true, Virgil."

As we rode up Old Nat she told me about how her father was a pimp turned preacher. How she has a sister named Porsche that went to Agnes Scott while she went to Spelman. How her father told her that upon graduation he expected her to go to seminary at The Candler School of Theology at Emory just as her sister was preparing to do. She told him no. He told her that he owned her car, her clothes, the money in her account and the Yaki in her head! He said that she would be a loving daughter and do as she was told. But it's true, two things can be true. She could be a loving daughter, and still not do as she was told.

Her roommate at Spelman, Gertrude, was dancing at an adult entertainment venue called Peaches on the weekend. Gertrude's stage name was BBS (Bubbling Brown Sugar), because let's face it if the DJ shouted next to the stage Gertrude, half of the men in there would have run for the door afraid their Memaw was about to start taking her clothes off. Alexus watched as Gertrude brought home what appeared to be a semester's worth of tuition every weekend. She thought to herself, my father may own those things but he doesn't own me. So in the words of Funkadelic, she took a chance and danced her way out of her constrictions.

She was twenty one at the time. She thought that dancing would be something temporary but money can make a five inch glass heel look and feel like a glass slipper. She said she took what felt like two twirls and suddenly she was about to turn thirty, and still dancing. Stripping is a young game and while thirty is still young to the rest of the world, it's old in stripper years. In the stripper world, when you turn thirty they're damn near ready to give you a subscription to AARP. Unfortunately glass heels and glass slippers both come with a midnight that makes carriages turn into pumpkins.

She said that she'd just been told that next month she'd no longer be in the weekend pole position. She was being moved to the early lunch shift. From there the adult entertainment path leads to The Claremont Lounge, where strippers go to die. It's like Florida for retirees, or Decatur for everyone. Then she said,

"Plus this is a weird time in the adult entertainment venue world. This social distancing got us giving lap dances six feet away from the patrons. Which is less than ideal. Many men, and women, have started going home to their wives. To someone they can actually touch. They also say the virus can live for days on hard surfaces. So no one wants to handle the pole, or a man's crotch. They say it can even live on money. So when anyone makes it rain I'm shooting the bills out of the air with a Lysol can that I keep strapped beneath my garter. It's like skeet. Well, I guess it's more like skeet skeet skeet skeet."

We both laugh and then I say,

"These are certainly strawn-jay times Ms. Alexus."

She half smiles and replies,

"Yes they are. You know, I'm thinking about going back to my roots.

Back to the church."

"Really?"

"Yeah. I'm thinking of teaching Liturgical Pole Dancing."

"Well that would be different."

"Yeah. I can teach em how to bus it open for the Lord. I might even save a few marriages along the way."

"Amen Miss Alexus. Amen."

"I was on my feet all night so I'm going to go sit down. Good talking to you Virgil. And if you're ever not a happily married man. Well..."

Miss Alexus winks, sticks her tongue out, says aaahhhhh, and twerks her way to her seat. I continue up Old Nat. I hope my father heard what I said before I was led down a road that ended with pole dancing in a pulpit. I hope I remember to speak to him more often now that I know he's here. I also hope that Gerald is not at the next bus stop.

The last thing I want or need today is to be engaged in conversation with a Hotep-trapboy. To be stuck in a chat with someone that is half Five Percenter, and half dime bagger. I crest the horizon just past The Crowe's Nest Megaplex and there he stands in all of his gold front glory. Gerald. Or as he is sometimes called, Gerald Jihad X Armstrong.

My mom once told me that a little bit of knowledge can be a dangerous thing. I don't think I truly understood that until I met Gerald. Gerald is all deep meditations, shallow conspiracy theories, mix-n-match religions, and unbridled confidence covered in patchouli oil. It's quite the combination. As is his name. He said he kept Gerald to honor his mother. The Jihad is to show his Muslim brothers that he's down to fight. The X is because he rejects his slave name. Armstrong is because he had to re-embrace his slave name or his father would have kicked him out of the basement where he lives. He often tells people to just call him Michael. I don't know.

Anyway, Gerald boards the bus dressed in clothes so oversized that it looks as if he's still trying to grow into them. He wears a black baseball cap, atop a red kufi, atop a black wave cap. Also, he's bald thus rendering the wave cap superfluous. He appears to have an A-frame t-shirt, often referred to as a wife beater, over a red t-shirt, I can only assume to match the kufi. Draped over all of that is a long white T-shirt with designer made holes in it. Gerald is notorious for wearing a pair of boxer briefs, under a pair of boxers, under a pair of basketball shorts, under a pair of very baggy jeans. The young man has more layers than an onion.

He often catches the bus near the closed and abandoned Wachovia on Old Nat. The one where someone spray painted the words, God Will, in front of Wachovia. When you say it out loud, with a bit of a southern inflection, it sounds like, God Will Watch Over Ya. Which is something I can't argue with.

Gerald Jihad X Armstrong, aka Michael, traps behind that abandoned bank alongside a few of his friends. Nothing serious it appears, just a little weed. He once told me that weed shouldn't be illegal because it's just a plant, and that the first marijuana plant grew from the grave of King Solomon. He also told me that the word marijuana is a combination of the name Mary as in The Virgin Mary, John the Baptist's name in Spanish, and Jah who art in heaven. Thus Mary-Juan-Jah. A trinity of sorts. He then theorized that, therefore marijuana in and of itself is immaculately conceived, a brother to Jesus, and God in its own right. So you cannot love Jesus, and God, and not love the stickiest of the icky. Full disclosure, and as I'm sure you've probably already figured out, he was incredibly high when he told me this.

I told him that I don't completely disagree. I think weed is less dangerous than alcohol but also I thought King Solomon was buried in a tomb. It's hard to grow anything in a stone tomb. I mean they very well could have had hydroponics back then I guess. Look at the hanging gardens of Babylon. Hell, I know a guy in East Point that grew Purp in his wife's she-shed. Listen, in biblical times they had a gentleman you might Noah-bout that built a boat so big that two of every animal got on board, so clearly they could have worked out how to grow weed in a tough spot. Also, was anyone calling John the Baptist, Juan? I mean clearly he, and especially Mary, were treated like poor people of color. You can't have your baby over here. You can't stay at the inn over there. I'll call a plague of ICE down on you. Would they have called him Juan and not have called her Maria? It should have either been MaryJohnJah or MariaJuanJah. I do, one hundred percent, agree that marijuana is a plant though.

Gerald told me that I was not up on the day's mathematics. That I needed to use my third eye, and my fourth one if it was available. He

34

informed me that I was falling for Trick-a-nomics and Trick-nology.

Gerald will definitely made-up-hybrid-word you to death if you let him. Once, while we were discussing the fact that Jiffy ain't cornbread he said to me, "Oh what a wicked web we weave when first we practice to deceive, to Diss-Eve," and then looked at me like, get it.

I said, "What the hell does that have to do with cornbread!"

Today however, Gerald boards with a wide smile and no words. Now this is odd. I was not looking forward to his nonsense talk but now that there is none, I kind of miss it.

So I say to him,

"Hey, hey Gerald. I hear that Donald Trump is trying to buy the German company that's going to manufacture the COVID-19 vaccine. So he will DON himself in billions of dollars while TRUMPing the disease, huh, huh."

Anyway, it's a weak attempt at Hotep talk but it's the best I can do. He doesn't say anything for a while. Then he looks at me and says,

"Sounds good Mr. Virgil."

Well now I'm really at a loss. Nothing gets Gerald's ankh-positive blood boiling like a good Donald Trump conspiracy theory. So I have to ask,

"Gerald are you, alright?"

Through a smile that lives in his eyes he says,

"Yeah. Actually, I'm better than alright."

"What's better than being alright? Being half left. Hahahaha."

I laugh alone. Gerald just continues to smile. He stares forward through the windshield of the bus like he sees something we don't on the horizon.

Then he says,

"What's better than alright is that my queen just told me she's pregnant. I'm going to be a father, Mr. Virgil."

Now my smile matches his.

"Well congratulations Gerald!"

From behind us comes the voice, and handless applause, of Miss Alexus,

"Yes Gerald, congrats!"

Gerald's chest seems to push up and out a bit more.

"Thank y'all. I just got the news like twenty minutes ago. Y'all are actually the first people I've told."

"We're honored Gerald. How are you feeling? You look like the Cheshire cat, that ate the Cheshire cat, that ate the canary."

"I don't know Mr. Virgil. I guess I feel happy, and scared, and nervous, but mostly happy. I've imagined this day but it's even more wonderful than what I imagined. It's like if someone told you what a rainbow looked like, you might be intrigued. If they drew you a rainbow, you'd have some idea of what it was. But if you saw with your own eyes a rainbow. You'd be amazed."

He continues,

"Thinking about being a father is like having it described to me. My queen telling me she's pregnant is like someone handing me a drawing of fatherhood. I imagine that when my child is born it will be like looking into the face of a rainbow."

I don't know what to say. This is the most sense Gerald has made since I've known him. I can't find any words but Alexus does.

"Funny thing about rainbows, some people get so lost searching for the pot of gold at the end that they miss the magic of the beginning. If I could tell my father anything, I'd tell him that once the rainbow is here you can't shape it into something it's not, and you can't make it be anything other than the colorful bridge across the sky, and generations, that it is. What you can do, however, is look for it after every storm, and know that everything is going to be alright in the end, pot of gold or not. What about you, Virgil. You're a father. Do you have any advice to give a father to be?"

I think Gerald and I are both struck by how poignant Alexus's words are. We both turn and look at her and each other.

There is just silence and then she says,

"What! I went to college! I'm a stripper, not an idiot. Uhm, Virgil eyes on the road please! We've got a father to be on board!"

I turn around and say over my shoulder,

"What the hell am I supposed to say after that Alexus! You've certainly hit us with some glass heel half full wisdom."

"I'd appreciate anything you have to say," Gerald says, his voice

37

full of sincerity.

"The only reason I get on this bus and debate with you Mr. Virgil is because you're one of the wisest men I know."

"Well damn it all to hell! No pressure."

Then I feel it. I feel the spirit of my father standing with me, and guiding me. I open my mouth and we speak with one voice.

"Know that the thing your child will want the most, is you. Your time, your attention, your direction, your encouragement, your love. There is no bicycle, pair of sneakers, or game system that will mean more to them in the long run. And the run is long. And they will trip and fall along the way. Just pick them up when they fall. Life moves so fast, remember to slow down and run alongside them when they stumble, and cheer them on when they hit their stride. Make a way and show them that life comes with choices. That they don't always have to eat the Cream of Wheat. There's oatmeal too."

I wipe tears away in the silence that lives after. I know what was said was just as much for me as it was for Gerald. Gerald breaks the silence.

"Thank you for that Mr. Virgil. For everything. The oatmeal part, that was weird though. And to think you had the nerve to criticize me for the cornbread thing."

We all laugh. They say misery enjoys company. So does joy.

Alexus gets off two stops later and Gerald rides with me to the end of the line. As he exits the bus I ask him if he knows what he'll name the child. He says that if it's a girl his queen likes the name Tracy but if it's a boy he'd like to name him Michael. Michael Armstrong. Gerald disappears up the ramp and into the MARTA station.

I take off my pink, lace, homemade bra-mask and reflect on the blessing it is, especially in these uncertain times, to have a community so diverse and varied. Homeless-ghost whispering geniuses, college educated adult venue entertainers, expectant Hotep fathers, and all those in between. A blessing. I also can't help but honor the hope that comes with a new life. Once talk of the baby began no one mentioned the coronavirus again. Life will go on, and so will the eighty-nine. It's essential. They're essential. I'm essential. That's who they are, and who I am.

Who are you?

# *That Masked Man*

## [a Tale from the 89 || True]

### *That Masked Man*
[a Tale from the 89 || True]


"The bus is free? The bus is free!? Ain't that a bitch! How the bus gone be something we ain't!"

He says this to no one in particular as he boards. He's tall. So tall he has to bow slightly, as if in reverence, as he enters the sanctuary of the number eighty-nine bus through its rear doors. His quip gets a few laughs, some muffled by masks, some not. He gets, in agreement, some head nods. It gives the impression that several people on the bus are listening to the same beat. He smiles wide. He's missing almost all of his back teeth which makes his grin seem somewhat equine. He pauses then opens his mouth even wider as if to say something else, but nothing as clever seems to reside beyond his front teeth, and back gums. Instead, he closes his mouth, sits, looks out of the window, and revels in his, albeit brief, comedic victory as the eighty-nine bus moves away from the College Park station.

We all sit physically distanced on what has always been a socially distanced bus ride. Ears filled with earbuds. Eyes filled with iPhones. We head south toward Old National Highway, together, separately, in silence.

COVID-19 has changed the rules of bus riding. Now we all must enter the bus via the back doors like it's the 1950s and we're trying to get a meal, or see a movie, or rent a room while Black. We're all Homer

Plessy. We're none of us Rosa Parks. The ghosts of those that are long gone, that were long suffering, and long denied seem to meet me face to face at the backdoor every time I board. As if to say, didn't we open doors for you? It sends a shiver down my spine, every time. Maybe, in true reverence, I too should bow like the tall equine smiler when I cross the threshold of the bus.

Every other bus seat has in it a yellow sticker, with a black chair at the center of a red circle, with a red line through it. It signifies that no one is to sit there. Redlining always lets you know where you're not supposed to be. Where the Blacks are not to be seated. The stickers are strategically placed to keep everyone six feet away from everyone else. They work, mostly.

Masks to help slow the spread of the novel coronavirus are appreciated but not mandated to ride the bus. The masked to unmasked ratio on the eighty-nine is about fifty-fifty. If the powers that be wanted people to wear masks they should have never said that the masks are to help others. They should have said, "The masks are to protect, YOU." People are much more into self than societal preservation.

There's one thing that people on the eighty-nine have always championed and preserved, however, and that's individual style and flair. This certainly has extended to the face masks. Almost as soon as people began wearing them nationwide, people on the eighty-nine started showing up with them bedazzled, airbrushed, and customized. There are some colorful and varied looks and messages on the masks. One young lady has what appears to be the bottom half of her face airbrushed on her mask. She looks like a comic book come to life. A gentleman just past the door sports a mask with a Nike symbol on the right side, and the words, Just Fuck It, on the other. I feel like there's a strong chance that it may not be an officially licensed product. A woman closer to the front has a drawing of a Black Betty Boop on her mask. I want to shout out, Esther Jones! I don't. I know that my shout would be muffled by my mask and probably not understood, even if heard. There's a Louis Vuitton mask, bandanas turned into masks (wild west bandit style), a mask with Tupac on it wearing a mask (meta), and plenty of just plain black masks like the one I'm wearing.

Then there are the people not wearing masks. Those that probably feel like corona can't do anything to them that the 2 for 2 from their favorite fast food restaurant hasn't already done. The most notable of the non-mask wearers is a White gentleman in a hospital gown. He is wearing no shoes. Footloose. He's got an assortment of grocery bags tied together and a pair of crutches flanking him as he eats voraciously. He eats from a plastic container, with his fingers, cantaloupe cut into cubes. The bus driver says something to him about his shoes. Footloose points to his crutches as his way of answering the bus driver's challenge. The bus driver then says there's no eating on the bus. Footloose shrugs, looks at the driver and keeps eating, as his way of answering the bus driver's challenge. The bus driver sighs, accepts the non-answers given, and keeps driving.

The exchange stays with me for a while because I've seen Black people put off of the bus for these same reasons: no shoes, and eating on the bus. A valid excuse, much less a point and a shrug, has never been accepted as an answer for such activity. I've watched Black people be threatened with, Do I have to call MARTA police!? I've watched Black people stand and exit the bus. I've watched them, left on the sidewalk, the roadside, the pages of history, as the bus pulls away. Maybe it's my anger and frustration with the current times we live in. Maybe it's that I'm still fighting back tears for Breonna Taylor, Oluwatoyin, George Floyd, Ahmad Arbery, and the list goes on, but I feel... irritated by the exchange. The bus pulls off and I settle into my non-redlined seat. I put on some music, lower my shoulders, and let my mind drift away.

I see it out of the corner of my eye. Footloose's arms are flailing about like sheets on a clothesline. His face is balled up like a fist. I take off my headphones. His maskless mouth is pointed and spewing obscenities like a firehouse. He froths like a dog with rabies, and spittle flies as he shouts. The veins in his neck are knotted like ropes. His eyes are wide. His pupils small. His eyebrows damn near lost in his hairline. I look in the direction that he's looking in, and I see her. A young Black woman wearing a blue baseball cap, and a green mask.

She has cheekbones so high no mask can hide them. Her eyes are dancing in what looks to be a mixture of confusion and fear. I see Oluwatoyin's face. I see the video of the young Black woman being thrown in a dumpster. I see the video of the young Black lady being knocked unconscious by a skateboard. I drop my backpack into the seat beside me. As I do this I see the gentleman across from me, no mask, just a look of boiling anger begin to move also. Just as we're standing another brother stands and then we hear a voice somewhere between a tenor and a baritone say,

"Who the fuck you think you talkin' to shawty!"

It's the Nike-Just-Fuck-It masked young man. He's one seat away from the woman in distress and closing the distance fast.

"Shawty, I said! Who the fuck you think you talkin' to!"

He looks to be in his mid to late twenties, or at least that's what his energy and attire suggest. He's not very tall or very wide, but his presence has suddenly filled the bus. Everyone falls silent. Even the engine sounds quieter. The bus driver says...nothing. Everything on the moving bus feels still.

Footloose, much like Equine-Smiler earlier, seems to be searching for something to say but finds no words. The Nike-Just-Fuck-It Masked Man moves closer and the woman that had been the target of Footloose's vitriol, says,

"It's okay. I think he's not well," her eyes say, don't get yourself into any trouble over me.

I can't help but think of how Black women in danger and distress will still extend themselves in an effort to protect us.

The Nike-Just Fuck It Masked Man says,

"He not so crazy he can't get his ass whipped on this bus! I see he ain't so crazy that he don't know when to shut the fuck up! He ain't that crazy!"

Quietly and slowly, as if not trying to trigger a Tyrannosaurus, Footloose reaches up and pushes the button for the next stop. He gathers his bags and crutches as The Nike-Just Fuck It Masked Man stands and watches him like a hawk. The bus comes to a stop in front of the Old National Kroger. Footloose stands to exit the bus. As he passes The Nike-Just Fuck It Masked Man he turns slightly as if to say something. The Nike-Just Fuck It Masked Man steps forward, his fists balled like Footloose's face had been, ready for whatever comes next. Footloose looks at his hands, then his face, exercises his right to remain silent, and exits the bus. Safely on the sidewalk, just as the bus doors close, Footloose begins to jump up and down on his "hurt" feet, yelling, and raving, and giving the bus and all of its occupants the finger.

The Nike-Just Fuck It Masked Man yells back,

"Yeah! Okay! But talk that shit from the curb tho!"

The bus pulls off. Everyone sits. The bus continues silently down Old National Highway.

# *Change Gone Come*

# *Come*

[a Tale from the 89 || True-ish]

# Change Gone Come
## [a Tale from the 89 || True-ish]

*10:15 a.m. || Godby Rd and Old National Hwy || Route 89 MARTA*

She boards the bus with her eyes fixed on the back seats. As she boards she exhales words that are immediately inhaled and swallowed before they can be heard. Words meant, maybe, just for herself. She wears blue jeans, and a white jacket with blue accents zipped all the way up. A rubber band pulls her hair back into an unkempt ponytail. Wisps of hair escape and stretch toward the ceiling as if waking from a long nap. From her lips dangles an unlit Newport that bounces like a symphony conductor's baton as she speaks her inaudible words. The corners of her mouth point to her feet and her feet are pointed toward the rear of the bus. She produces a well-worn MARTA card, taps it against the fare collector, and moves swiftly toward the seat her eyes have been on the whole time.

"Hey. HEY!" comes a call from the bus driver. His words find nothing but the back of her head as she moves steadily away from him.

"HEY! You don't have enough money on your card!"

Her stride never slows. Her head never turns to acknowledge his claim. She moves purposefully toward her goal.

"Hey!" he growls again.

The bus driver reaches into his pocket, pulls a cell phone, and begins dialing a number he seems to know by heart. The woman settles into the rear bus seat her eyes have never left. Her shoulders relax. Her head rests against the cool window pane. She closes her eyes and, for the first time since boarding the bus, stops mumbling.

The bus driver hangs up the cell phone and shouts,

"You either pay, exit the bus, or go to jail! The police are on the way!"

She opens her eyes, wide, and searching. She sits up. She sits perfectly still as her eyes dance around the bus wildly. The driver addresses the bus,

"I'm sorry folks we're not going to be able to leave until the police get here!"

A gentleman near the front addresses the bus driver,

"Come on folk! I can't be late again! I'm gone lose my job."

A lady a few seats behind him turns and addresses the woman,

"Come on now! Get off the bus!"

Others start to grumble and voice their displeasure, the ire rising.

I say to the lady,

"How short are you on the fare?"

Eyes that had been searching fall on me and go still. A voice that usually only speaks to itself reaches across the seats and replies,

"The whole thing."


*10:00 a.m. || Flat Shoals Rd and Old National Hwy || Route 89 MARTA [Fifteen minutes prior]*


The eighty-nine rounds the Kroger and slows to a halt. I'm tempted to wait for the one-eighty-nine bus. The two bus routes, just like their route numbers, only differ slightly. Headed south their routes go their separate ways once they pass the Kroger. Coming north, once they reach Flat Shoals and Old Nat, their routes become one and the same. I usually take the one-eighty-nine in the morning headed north. It's quieter, and more relaxed. I don't have to worry about six inch clear heels stepping on my shoes or hear about wild conspiracy theories that may or may not involve dogs. Yep, usually I wait on the one-eighty-nine, but on this balmy morning the eighty-nine arrives first and swings open doors that release the warmth of grandma's oven.

I board the warm bus with $2.50 in quarters in hand to pay the fare. I tap my card against the fare collector and it reads, *accepted*, which means I get to keep my change. I walk to the back of the bus thinking, that was odd. I don't ever put extra money on my MARTA card. I pay as I go. What if I get hit by a bus, or have a heart attack and die? MARTA ain't fittin' to keep my extra two-fifty. No sir. So, there is no reason there should be a free fare on my card, but who am I to look a gift iron horse in the mouth. They say, thank God for things big and small. So I thank God and I put on some Biggie Smalls. I tuck the change back into my pocket, take one of the few empty seats near the rear of the bus, and look out of the window at streets I know all too well.

*10:17 a.m. || Godby Rd and Old National Hwy || Route 89 MARTA*
*[seventeen minutes later]*

I say to the lady,
"How short are you on the fare?"

In a voice that is a whisper if it's anything she replies,
"The whole thing."

I reach into my pocket remembering the fare in change that's still there as a result of my unexpected free ride. I fish it out and say,
"Here you go. No one should have to go to jail over pocket change."

Her eyes soften. She seems on the verge of tears as her hand, shaking, reaches across the seats and takes the money from mine.

A gentleman seated near us shouts up to the bus driver,
"Hey! Hey folk! She got the money buddy! No one should have to go to jail over pocket change boi."

Funny, I've heard that somewhere before.

A few other people take up his championing of her cause. Some of her now champions had previously argued for her expulsion from the bus. Amazing how quickly tides, ideas and stances can change.

She makes her way to the front, pays the fare and beats a hasty retreat back to her seat. The bus driver pulls the cell phone from his pocket and calls off the red dogs.

The woman whispers over to me,
"Mister, you gave me $2.75 here's your other quarter."

I say,
"It's okay, you can keep it."

"No sir, I appreciate what you done. It's yours," is her reply.

"My name is Dometrice," she says as she places the quarter back in my hand.

She smiles for the first time and I shake her hand. I actually already know more about Dometrice than I should. I know her full name, date of birth, and according to the hospital band on her wrist her case number is 1846594. There is a picture of her on her wristband. In the picture she's wearing the same clothes she has on now.

She may have released herself on her own recognizance. She may have nothing to wear but what she is currently wearing. I'm not sure. The one thing I am sure of is that she shouldn't have to go to jail over pocket change. The bus pulls off and eventually makes it to the station.

I stand to leave and she says,

"Mister?"

I say, "Yes?"

She says, "I will take that other quarter if you're not going to use it."

I give her the quarter and exit the bus. As I walk to the train I think to myself, what if I had been charged for my ride? What if I had taken the 189? What if? Then I thank God that I hadn't, and that I didn't.

# *Buttermilk*

## [a Historical Fiction]

# *Buttermilk*
## [a Historical Fiction]

Some say it was a red hot fire that burned down the not-so-old Fourth Ward in 1917. Those of us that know the truth of it know it was white hot hate. Oh, they had the water, the hoses, the men, the power, the manpower to put out the fire (a fire that raged for ten hours and consumed over three hundred acres of mostly Black businesses). Oh yes, they had the tools but what they didn't have was the will, want, need, and desire; that was until it started reaching the homes and businesses of White Folk. Then suddenly it was a crisis, a catastrophe, a fire that had to be stopped at all cost. By the end what it cost Black Folk was all of everything we'd struggled for, fought for, and built in the Fourth Ward. And if you, me, we tried to go back to the cooling embers of what used to be your, my, our home, and sift through the rubble of our lives for what little was left, we were called looters by angry voices that lived at the other end of quiet badges with guns anxious to speak. Can you imagine that? Being accused of stealing YOUR things, of looting YOUR own life.

After the hungry fire ate its fill, the few White Folk that found themselves displaced received compassion, prayer, and tents provided by the city in Piedmont Park. The now homeless Black Folk (estimated to be roughly ten thousand in number) received prayer from other Black Folk. Insurance companies paid out to White Folk quicker than you can say, Nathaniel Edwin Harris. Those dignified, and newly indemnified, White families and individuals took that money and used it to plant seeds that grew into lasting roots on Atlanta's Northside. They put the fire behind them and let its glow light a path forward toward a bright future. Conversely, insurance companies denied the claims of Black Folk faster than you can say, Jump Jim Crow. The fruit of our labors had not withered but instead been incinerated on the vine. We stared down the barrel of a future as grey as the ash that floated, like summer dandelion fluff, for weeks through the streets of the Fourth Ward.

Like the dust of what was, we eventually settled. Once we did we looked around, got our bearings, took in our surroundings, and found ourselves in Mississippi Bottom. Never heard of it? Not many have.

Mississippi Bottom was an undeveloped area that, on a city map, rested just north of the Fourth Ward and just south of Piedmont Park. In our hearts, at the time, it was just north of nowhere we wanted to be and just south of everything we'd ever hoped for. It was no man's land. Literally. Mississippi Bottom was made up of dirt lots, and dirt roads that had no names and no drains. Hell, we got there before electricity did.

We took whatever wood we could scavenge and salvage (not loot) from homes that were once ours and used it to Phoenix a new community from the flames. We cobbled together a shadow of yesterday. A faded photo of what we used to be. A quiet echo of who we were. That's what Mississippi Bottom was, just the Cliff's Notes of a people.

When it rained in The Bottom, and it seemed to rain a lot (as if God himself wept for our conditions), the rain water would river through the cracks and crevices of the salvaged wood and shingles, and wash free what seemed to be the everlasting remnants of soot and ash that lived there. The ash in the wood, evocative of blood on a politician's hands, could never be completely washed clean. The ashen rainwater would run from the roofs like lemmings off a cliff, and turn the dirt in the roads, in the yards, and on the porches into swirling white mud. When the rain stopped the water would stand as still as the grave, and stagnate, putrefy, go sour.

The white swirly mud looked exactly like what was leftover after milk had been churned to butter, and smelled like laundry gone old. This fetid, motionless, mulatto mud that stuck to your shoes, to your clothes, to your life, is why most people think Mississippi Bottom was over time dubbed Buttermilk Bottom. Those who know the truth of it know different.

I was told but I can't remember his real name. No one can seem to anymore. He's been described as tall and short, as dark and fair, as stout and thin. He's been described as not a man at all but a beautiful woman, or even a not so beautiful woman. What everyone can agree on is that he, she, they was known in the pre-fire Fourth Ward for making a way out of no way. For patch-working together miracles. They could take the wood scraps from the lumberyard and make you a chifferobe better than anything you could find at market. Take those couple of black eyed peas, that half a piece of fatback, the good part of the onion you had left, and get your John to Hoppin'. They could take the stone the builders rejected and make you a forever home.

Mr. Richardson said one spring, not for love nor money could he get the crops in his field to dig their feet into the earth and stretch their arms toward the sun. Then they came over chewing on a camphor root with a small piece of cotton in their hand. They walked that field for a whole day, whispered words no one could understand to someone or something no one could see, and touched that cotton to everything. After two weeks, and a couple of good rains, Mr. Richardson had the best crop he'd ever known.

Miss Ethel had a mule that wouldn't mind, or rather had a mind of its own. They came over chewing on a piece of sugar cane. They extended a steady hand palm up toward the mule, and approached it slowly. They pressed their forehead to the mule's for about a minute, and whispered words no one could understand to someone or something no one could see. Miss Ethel said, "I had nary 'nother day of trouble out of that mule." There is story after story after story about him, her, them making the wrong right. Making the crooked straight. Making something sweet from sour times. People took to calling them Buttermilk.

They say on Monday, May twenty-first, in the year of our Lord nineteen and seventeen at ten in the morning Buttermilk was down on Edgewood looking at Mr. Pernell's new motor coach. A model T Touring he'd bought brand new for four-hundred dollars. This was back when four hundred dollars was FOUR HUNDRED DOLLARS. Back when Black Folk were lucky to make fourteen dollars a week.

It was hot that Monday even for Atlanta which was, and is, known for a heat that could knock a strong man down. As the sun moved toward the height of the sky's ceiling, the wind kicked up like a mare with a burr beneath its saddle pushing that lard hot air to every corner of the Fourth Ward. With every gust it felt like the Devil himself was blowing his un-mouthwashed morning breath in your face. Stirring up aggravation, irritation, tension.

At eleven in the morning, that blistering wind at their back pushing them forward, the police arrived in the Fourth Ward. Patrolling. Controlling. Keeping the piece as it was called by some. They walked the neighborhood, taking up the entirety of the sidewalk, their heads held high like they were the kings of everything. They numbered three. Three officers with their eyes scanning for anything out of place, in a place where Black people could be anything. Their feet pounded the pavement while their hands, out of habit, rested lazily on their pistols. At eleven-thirty that morning they spotted Mr. Pernell, Buttermilk, and tragically the brand new motor coach.

Tensions in Atlanta between Black Folk and White Folk (the police were always White Folk) had been high since the 1906 massacre of Black Folk up at Five Points. Five Points had become the center of Black life and wealth in pre-1906 Atlanta. The massacre, in September of '06, proved that the only thing White Folk in Atlanta hated more than poor Black Folk, was Black Folk that weren't poor.

At Eleven-thirty two a.m. the police approached Mr. Pernell and

Buttermilk. They asked, rather demanded, "Whose car is this!?" Buttermilk stood silently chewing on a mint leaf as Mr. Pernell proudly, but nervously, claimed ownership. The police instantly claimed the vehicle to be stolen. They moved to arrest Mr. Pernell, confiscate the vehicle and return it to its rightful owner (which would have probably been one of them. Keeping the piece). Mr. Pernell was no troublemaker. He wasn't known as one to rouse rabble. No. What he was, was a man that had more taken from him in his lifetime than he could bear to part with, and he was going to part with not another thing. Through a shaky but firm voice he let them know that they would not be taking his motor coach.

At eleven-thirty seven that morning the police began moving toward Mr. Pernell, gaining ground as he stood his. Their raised voices found the ears of the good people of the Fourth Ward who then came out to stand with Mr. Pernell and Buttermilk. A small crowd formed. No one knows for sure who fired the first shot but any and all in attendance agreed that only the police were armed. People took cover as the first of many shots was fired. At eleven-forty, one of the bullets fired sparked off the street and landed atop the wooden shingles of a home. With the oppressive heat and constant wind, it didn't take much to turn that spark into a flame, into a fire, into a blaze. The roof caught at eleven-forty two and by noon a full on, all consuming, fire was racing and jumping its way toward Sweet Auburn.

Mr. Pernell took a bullet to the leg in the melee and was taken away by community members to be cared for. Buttermilk however got lost in the shuffle. One minute he was there and the next he was gone. Some said he ran for safety. Some said he'd been shot and killed. No one knew. All that was known, and what had everyone's full attention, was that there was a fire running like sixteen year old Harry Edward across the rooftops of the Fourth Ward.

The path of the fire took it north up Jackson St. where Mrs. May's restaurant stood helplessly and hopelessly in its path. It gobbled up her store like a piece of penny candy and rushed to Wheat Street. Wheat St. Baptist church was consumed whole as if inhaled in one breath by the flames. The inferno sprinted across Highland leaving what appeared to be a forest of burnt chimneys in its wake as it crossed Forrest toward Ponce. Wood, heat, and wind fueled the fire as it devoured everything as far south as Decatur Street, north as Fifth, west as Bedford, and east as Randolph.

The Atlanta Fire Department was alerted. People will tell you that they were slow to respond because there were other fires in the city. That's what they'll tell you. Those who know the truth of it though will tell you that firefighters showed up with no fire fighting equipment. They showed up in uniform, stood, and watched the Fourth Ward cross streets burning like they were at a family bar-b-que. Ten hours later ninety percent of everything in the Fourth Ward was gone. More was destroyed by fire in those few hours than all of what Sherman put the torch to in Atlanta as he marched to the sea. They say matter can neither be created nor destroyed. The hell they say. I tell you now, the things that matter can absolutely be destroyed.

A few weeks later Mississippi Bottom was created out of necessity. It was initially called Mississippi as a reminder to ourselves to not get too comfortable. To remember that we'd escaped terrible conditions in the past and would certainly break free of these. Hammers were swung with purpose. Saws were pulled and pushed to a sad rhythm. Nails were driven deep into charred wood. A community was built, but it wasn't as easy as all that.

People would speak of being in the midst of creating a frame for a house and running out of nails by night's end. They'd leave, return in the morning, and there'd be a bucket of nails on the ground and the strong scent of camphor hanging in the air. Somedays by noon they'd come to the end of their salvaged wood. The work crew would break for lunch, come back in an hour or so, and find that they now had more than enough wood. More wood than they'd started with. Then someone would sniff out the aroma of sugar cane moving on the breeze. Food and the smell of mint would sometimes appear where there had previously been neither. No one could explain it, but they began offering prayers, whispered words no one could understand to someone or something no one could see, in response to these miracles. These blessings. Then one day Miss Mickey found in her makeshift home a cobbled together chifferobe that was as good as anything you could find at the market. That's when people started calling it Buttermilk Bottom.

Buttermilk Bottom was a community making something sweet out of something sour. A people churning through life and using every drop of what they made, created, and conjured. It was a home for folk tall and short, dark and fair, stout and thin. Buttermilk Bottom's breadth, width, and sheer acreage could be measured in inches, yards, and miles, but its heart, tenacity, and magic knew no limits; and still knows no limits if you know the truth of it.

On January twenty-eighth, in the year of our Lord twenty and fourteen, Rhonda Williams was stuck in the bumper to bumper, motionless traffic of I-85 during Atlanta's Snowpocalypse. She tells of the shiver that ran down her spine as her car sputtered out of gas, and the heat shut off. As the sun dipped behind the horizon the temperatures dipped well into the teens. Rhonda zipped her jacket up as tightly as she could, prayed she'd see the sun rise again, and fell asleep. She woke a few hours later in a full sweat. The car was awash in heat. The gas gauge read full. The gas tank hadn't been full when she'd left that morning. She'd dreamt that someone had put their forehead against hers and whispered words as she slept. The surname Williams was Rhonda's through marriage. Her maiden name was Pernell. Her great great grandfather once owned the first motor coach in the Fourth Ward.

As part of the non-violent, student led, telepathic sit-in movement for planetary rights, Hezekiah Richardson logged-in from a secure location and seated himself in the frontal lobe of all of the patrons of Atlanta's Intergalactic Space Station. The date was March fifteenth, in the year of our Lord thirty and forty six. The people who were in the space station's cafeteria for lunch were less than pleased. Pointed slurs and heated threats were hurled at him and four other activist students telepathically as they sat resolute in their effort to agitate for equality throughout the universe. The violent thoughts of the patrons soon turned into violent actions. Mind Monitors were alerted. They tracked the poorly encrypted signal of Hezekiah and his cohorts to their location and dispatched Thought Police. The cops breached the building and went old school, raining fists and wands down on the small student group. They were told that arresting them involved more official duties and decrees than the officers cared to carry out, but if they engaged in another telepathic sit-in it would be their last. All of the students returned to their domi-cubes. They went to bed that night beaten, broken, and battered, but woke without so much as a single bruise. Hezekiah upon examining himself found the remnants of an ancient material known as cotton where one of his cuts should have been. Had been. He contacted his friends and discussed conducting another sit-in but with better encryption. Then he had a better idea still. They all got dressed, ordered a shared-shuttle, and soon arrived in person at Atlanta's Intergalactic Space Station. As they entered the space station's cafeteria Hezekiah chewed on a mint leaf. They sat down, set their feet, squared his shoulders, cuffed themselves ankle, wrist, and mind to each other, and in a voice that felt greater than their own asked for five glasses of something they weren't even sure existed, buttermilk.

# *Pluto*

[The King Stays on the Board || True-ish]

### *Pluto*
## [The King Stays on the Board || True-ish]

He walked into Woodruff Park slowly, like a man with time on his side. In one hand he held a zip-lock bag full of chess pieces and in the other a clock. The energy of the park was frenetic. Manic. The opposite of his. It was a summer day just past noon. The time of day when shadows fold in on themselves. People moved through every corner of this unexpected green space that lived like an oasis nestled between the busy streets, glass buildings, and sirens of downtown Atlanta.

On this day, like most, people in the park played music and danced. Others just sat on the grass, their hands in the earth and their faces to the sky soaking up the sun. Men and women in business suits hurried through the park en route to lunches and meetings. A cadre of park regulars played dominos, cards, scrabble, and of course chess. The park buzzed like a bee hive and smelled of midday sweat, baked concrete, and free two-day-old chicken wings. On this day the chess tables, and the bellies of the chess players, were all full. The smiles were ubiquitous and the trash talk constant.

He moved through the crowd like a shark's fin through open water as he slowly approached a table near the center of the park. None of the tables had owners, but it was known and understood that this particular table was his. He was a golden brown man dressed in a suit from a time long gone. A double breasted tan blazer with gold buttons. Navy trousers with starched creases that were so sharp they could cut

67

inflation. A snow white dress shirt with gold cufflinks, and a flared collar that sat outside of, and atop, the jacket's lapels. The suit and shirt were all made of a lightweight breathable cotton. The top two buttons of the shirt lay open revealing a gold chain nestled in mostly gray chest hair. He wore spats over brogues and set his heel with every stride as if goose stepping. The light cotton suit still seemed too warm for Atlanta's midday-summer heat, but he wasn't sweating. Not a single drop.

Voices whispered as he floated through the park

"It's Pluto."

"Oh shit! Pluto in the park."

"Money game Pluto!"

He acknowledged none of the comments. He gripped his pieces and clock tightly, and walked unhurriedly with his head high and a copy of the *Atlanta Journal Constitution* tucked beneath his right arm. By the time he reached "his" table the two men that had been playing there found somewhere else to be.

Pluto smoothed his trousers, sat down, crossed his legs, and draped the newspaper over his knee. He gently placed the clock beside the checkered pattern already carved into the table, and poured the chess pieces from the zip-lock bag. He sat up both sides of the board with meticulous care ensuring each piece was exactly in the center of the square. Once satisfied with the placement of the pieces he pushed some buttons on the clock, and then he sat out a sign written on a piece of cardboard that read, "3 to 1 for 5+ per." Meaning that he would allow you to put three minutes on your side of the chess clock while he only put one minute on his, and you'd be playing for five dollars or more per game. Pluto picked up the paper from his knee and began reading.

It didn't take long for player after player to take up the challenge. Some thought they could actually win, some just wanted to say they played against Pluto the chess park legend. He played everyone that sat across from him—no matter who you were or your reason for visiting the park—with indiscriminate expertise and ferocity. Pluto's mind and hand moved with a speed and agility that seemed to border on precognition. A player would pick up a piece to move it and Pluto, seeming to know what the player was going to do, would pick up his piece and move as well. The player would hit the clock and Pluto would hit the clock almost simultaneously. This happened so quickly that often no time would come off Pluto's clock. The game would be over in a blink either by checkmate or expired time, and the money changing hands under the table seemed to only go one way. To Pluto.

In one hundred and eighty seconds he beat nearly everyone that dared take a seat, until there were no more takers. As he sat reading his paper and smoking a cigarette like a man unwinding after a long day of work, I heard someone ask him about his game, his strategy, and why he would put himself at such a disadvantage.

He answered,
"You won't believe what your mind can do when under pressure and properly motivated. Why take ten, or even five minutes to do something that I can do in sixty seconds if I really try?"

As he answered he scooped his pieces back into the zip-lock bag, tucked his paper beneath his right arm, picked up his clock, smoothed his trousers, and began walking out of the park just as slowly as he'd entered it. Like a man with time on his side.

# *Obama Phone*

## [The King Stays on the Board || Fiction]

## Obama Phone
[The King Stays on the Board || Fiction]


There they were. They'd always been there in small but ever growing numbers. Pushed to the side like unwanted peas on a child's plate. Pushed beyond the margins like a toddler coloring outside the lines. Pushed into forgotten alleys, abandoned doorways, and under bridges like trolls that eat gruff billy goats. They were called un-housed, people experiencing homelessness, home insecure, and whatever other new phrase created by liberal allies so that they could feel better about themselves ruled the moment. They were everywhere, but still invisible. Their extended hands unseen. Their cardboard signs unread. Their existence erased like they were never sons, or daughters, or fathers, or mothers, or loved, or missed. But they were there, just beneath the surface, irritating the body politic like an ingrown toenail. Here's the thing about ingrown toenails though, if not treated, if allowed to grow, they fester, and become infected. They can cost you your toe, your foot, your whole leg. And without a leg to stand on the body politic, falls.

Brian worked in an office just off Woodruff Park, in downtown Atlanta. He'd worked in that office for a decade. He was an accountant. Accounting was a great job for him because he was a creature of order. He craved it. If there was one fish and two fish then there had to be a red fish and a blue fish. Although he could accept that numbers could be irrational, he could not accept that he could be. He'd eaten the same tuna salad sandwich, with the crusts cut off, for lunch the last five years. (For the previous five years it had been egg salad sandwiches, but then his doctor began discussing his cholesterol.) When Brian's jeans, or shoes, or shirts wore out he bought the same brands in the same sizes. He'd walked the same route from his apartment to the office for the last ten years. His home was in order. His finances were in order. His life was in order. He'd have it no other way. People used words like obsessive, compulsive, autistic, and high-functioning to describe him. He'd never been tested. He didn't know. He just knew that the right edge of the coffee table in his living room sat at true north, and didn't understand why everyone's didn't.

Brian was never good at talking to people or making friends. People used words like stand, offish, social, anxiety, and disorder to describe him. He didn't know. He just knew that people didn't find the things he found interesting, interesting. Conversely he just couldn't make himself care about the real housewives of wherever, or that the Knicks had lost to the Braves had lost to the Penguins had lost to the... So he kept to himself and listened. People used words like eavesdropping, ear hustling, and listening Tom to describe him. He didn't know.

Every day on his walk to and from work he'd see mostly the same people at the same time. People in power suits power walking their way to work. People without a pan or a handle, panhandling. Bike couriers. Students. Mostly the same people.

One morning he saw something different. Something out of order. He saw people power suit walking their way to work, bike couriers, and students, but there was no one panhandling. No extended hands. No cardboard signs. Every so often this would happen. Every so often the city would do Quality of Life Policing. This is where the police force is asked to arrest the people deemed undesirable for things like jaywalking, or congregating, or sleeping. They clear the streets because the President, or the Olympics, or the World Cup is coming, and they don't want strangers thinking they don't keep good house. This wasn't that though. The people that panhandle were still there. They were gathered on the corner of Peachtree and Edgewood staring silently at a man as he spoke. Brian had seen the man before. Had seen him for almost a decade. He was an affable and well-liked panhandler and card hustler in Woodruff. He was known to shout to beautiful women as they walked across the park, "I didn't know the sun rose twice a day!" Most days he was just trying to pull together enough money to cover a shelter fee. Most people think that homeless shelters are free, and many are—to a point. But after a few weeks stay some shelters begin charging a fee ranging from five to ten dollars. Whether he raised the fee or not the man always had a smile on his face and most days you could hear his voice echoing across the park, "I didn't know the sun rose twice a day!"

This day was different. The man wasn't smiling. He was speaking, but his voice wasn't booming across the park, rather it was just loud enough to keep those in front of him enrapt. Brian couldn't hear what was being said but he could tell by the passion in the man's gesticulations that he meant what he was saying. This was odd. This was out of order. What was even odder was that everyone listening was quiet, still, homeless, and recording every word being said with a small black phone.

That day in the break room, while eating his tuna salad sandwich, he heard some of his co-workers laughing as they watched a video on

74

their y-phones.

Brian could hear the voice on the video,

"... Every day. Every day our numbers are growing."

The voice in the video was that of a man. He wasn't shouting but speaking clearly and with conviction. Some of the words seemed to hiss out like air from a punctured tire. In Brian's mind he imagined the speaker speaking through clenched teeth.

"There are more of us living on the street than there are downtown police. More of us trying to find a way than people trying to find solutions. There are more of us locked up each night for just trying to survive than there is room to lock us up. They are pushing us past the margins, and when the margins collapse the center won't hold. Once the bubble is burst the center won't hold. To paraphrase Yeats, 'When things fall apart; the center cannot hold.'"

Brian's co-workers stopped the video. They laughed as they critiqued the man's clothes, his hair, his teeth or lack thereof. They called him Martin Loofah Clean, and Huey Peed his Pants. They talked about everything except what the man had said. Had they not heard him? Had they not heard the conviction in his voice? The substance of his argument? Had they not heard the rapt silence of the audience? The rapt silence. Brian finished his sandwich, went to his desk, and scoured the internet until he found the video. He realized instantly that this is what was being recorded as he walked to work. This was the sermon being given to the congregation at the corner of Peachtree and Edgewood.

On his walk home Brian looked to the corner and there he was, still speaking. His audience had grown considerably since this morning.

More of the city's forgotten, listening, nodding in agreement, and recording. The usual hustle, bustle, and noise of the park were gone. The card and chess games had ceased. The daily order of the park had been disrupted. Brian's right hand began to twitch. He didn't do well with change. With disruption. With disorder.

Every day as he walked to and from work the crowd grew. It went from just the corner to half the park. The from half the park to the whole park. The space adjacent to the park, by the water wall at Peachtree and Auburn, began to serve as an overflow. The man speaking had no amplification so Brian wondered how he was being heard. Then he realized that some of the people nearest the man were recording, and others livestreaming. The people not close enough to hear were watching on their cells and listening through headphones. For almost two city blocks the man's voice, speaking with measured passion, was the only barely audible sound. The voice of one calling in an urban wilderness.

As the recordings made the rounds through social media people used words like, hilarious, important, shameful, and poignant to describe the videos. Brian didn't know. He sat in the break room, ate his sandwich, and listened daily to what was being said not even fifty yards from his office window. The man's videos were made into Reels, and Tik-Toks. They were spoofed and dueted. The name that stuck with him on social media was #TheParkObama and the people listening were called #TheBlackPandlerMovement. The videos and hashtags went viral but very few people seemed to really hear what was being said. Instead of concentrating on the words the overwhelming question seemed to be, where and how did all of those homeless people get those phones?

Brian wondered this too, but where many wondered, guessed, and conspiracy theorized, Brian did what so few seemed willing to do. He looked it up. One evening while sitting at the right, true north, edge of his coffee table he discovered the Lifeline Program. It was established in 1985 to help poor people pay their phone bills, or offer free phone service. This was during the Reagan era, well before cellphones came to power. This was back when people memorized lists of phone numbers, called people from an analog line, and could only walk and talk as far as the cord of the phone would allow. In 2009 under President Obama the antiquated Lifeline Program was updated. People receiving certain government services, Medicaid and Medicare, or with income below certain levels qualified for a reduced cost, or free, cell phone. People who had been cut off from the world in many regards were now given a window into these modern days and times. Those people affectionately called these new windows, these new phones, Obama Phones. In honor of the President that made it possible.

Under the subsequent Presidents the program was paid little attention. It was a budget line that got funded every few years. That funding was used to upgrade the phones. Where the original Obama Phones were just simple black flip-phones, the current variety were sleek black smart phones. This upgrade took people from only being able to make calls and send texts, to being able to record videos, do livestreams, and most importantly, post them. Brian read all he could about the Lifeline Program and around 10 p.m. he fell asleep on his couch, the screen on his laptop still aglow. He always tucked himself neatly into bed at 9 p.m. and woke promptly at 5 a.m. He never set an alarm. It was the order of things. So when he woke the next morning, on the couch, at 6:30 a.m., his right hand began to tremble.

Brian showered and dressed hurriedly trying to get back on schedule. He made his lunch, and threw it into a bag. On his way out of the door he bumped into the living room table, jostling it slightly. He looked at it and then looked at his watch knowing he was behind. He rushed out the door leaving the right edge of the table not at true north. He walked briskly and contemplated going back and righting the table, but knew he was already behind on the day. Three blocks away from Woodruff Park he encountered the first of the stragglers. They were staring at their phones, headphones on, listening and walking toward the park. By the time he got to Hurt Park, two blocks away from Woodruff, he was in the thick of it. People stood shoulder to shoulder their feet covering every inch of Hurt Park. People lined the sidewalks leading from Hurt to Woodruff. They'd walk until the crush of people would allow no more forward movement, and then they'd just stand, stare at their phones, and listen. Brian was forced to walk in the street and dance between the cars. When he reached Woodruff he could tell by the orientation of the people's heads and bodies that the man dubbed #TheParkObama was speaking on the corner, but there were so many people you couldn't even see him now.

The Mayor sought to move the man and his congregants to a place called not-downtown-Atlanta. Mayors of the surrounding not-Atlanta towns were vehemently against this. The governor offered the Mayor the National Guard to clear the streets and parks of downtown. It was an election year and the Mayor didn't like the look, or subsequent

78

loss of votes, that would come with the military and their rifles and camouflaged vehicles rolling through downtown Atlanta and pushing a vulnerable population to who knows where. The news would eat him alive and the polls would pronounce him dead. Conservative pundits said, "The Mayor needs to crack some heads before this gets any further out of hand!" Liberal pundits cited Occupy Wall Street and the right to peacefully assemble. People in the middle just went on with their daily lives like nothing was happening.

Brian wanted to go on like nothing was happening, but he was behind in his day and couldn't seem to catch up. He arrived late to work. He subsequently left work late as well. He didn't even eat his tuna salad sandwich, which he threw away before heading home. When he got to the lobby of his office building he could barely get out of the front door. People were everywhere. As far as the eye could see. Brian wondered if #TheParkObama ever slept. Did he eat? Was he just speaking incessantly? Brian pushed his way home through the crowd, which was now four city blocks deep in all directions. The breadth of homelessness was on full display. This many people. Blocks and blocks, as far as the eye could see. The crowd had grown to just a few blocks short of his apartment. Spray painted on the sidewalk in front of his building were the words, THE CENTER CANNOT HOLD! Brian didn't know. He stepped over the writing and entered the building.

The city was paralyzed. Within a week Brian couldn't leave his apartment. The news began showing city after city where the streets were flooded with silent homeless persons. They were all listening to their phones. They were all listening to the same man. What had started as a speech on the corner of Peachtree and Edgewood had reached every corner of the nation. No one knew what to do. There didn't seem to be any demands or desire to negotiate. There was just this growth that was happening just beneath the nation's skin.

Brian sat at his living room table, which he'd never bothered to put back in place, and with shaking hands he ate an egg salad sandwich with the crust still on. He wasn't sure what was going to happen next but he felt keenly aware that the nation was looking at the dawning of something new, something different, something out of order. It was noon but as he stared out his apartment window at the ever growing mass of people he thought, I didn't know the sun rose twice a day.

# *Mourning Joe*

[The King Stays on the Board ||
True-Enough]

## Mourning Joe
[The King Stays on the Board || True-Enough]


Calling Joe loud would be a misnomer, an understatement of epic proportion. It would be like calling the noon day sun on a clear day a bit bright, or calling my two-tone 2002 Mercury Sable somewhat unreliable. The noon day sun is brilliant, my Mercury Sable is trash, and Joe is loud as fuck. A cacophonous mess. I mean, a bullhorn would tell him to keep it down.

Not only is Joe loud, he's also a passionate gesticulator. That sounds dirtier than it is. What it means is, when he's speaking, at volumes clearly meant to communicate with aliens in space, he also flails his arms around wildly. He looks like a desperate hitchhiker on a dark lonely road flagging down a car in a B horror movie. Like a Spirit Airlines flight attendant on meth giving a disjointed safety brief. Don't ask how I know what that last one looks like, just trust me.

Joe is just tall enough to not be considered tall at all. His growth cycle came to an abrupt halt in the ninth grade leaving him stranded in that nebulous, tall-for-a-boy but not-so-tall-for-a-man, area a few inches below six feet. This doesn't stop him from claiming he's six-two. A claim that is usually met with an up and down eye assessment, the cocking of a head, and the question, but are you though?

He's color struck that Joe. Color struck in so much as he finds the complexion of whatever man is currently popular with women in Black America, striking. He admires it because women desire it and so he purports to be it. When Dijmon Hounsou was all the rage Joe wrote in his Black Planet profile that he was chocolate/dark-skinned. If you or someone you know had a Black Planet account you (and them) probably need to think about reducing the sodium in your diet and exercising more regularly. The second Maxwell was ascendant Joe let his hair grow out and told people in internet chat rooms that he was caramel complected. If you or someone you know used to frequent internet chat rooms you (and them) probably need to schedule a colonoscopy. When El Debarge stood atop the mountain not only was Joe light-skinned, he was supposedly Puerto Rican. Even El Debarge is not Puerto Rican. Joe is a chameleon, but in name only. He can't actually change colors.

Lastly, Joe is a tough guy. But mostly in rooms filled with not-so-tough guys. In a room of kittens he's a roaring, charging, lion. In a room of lions he's a nervous, still, gazelle.

He's a regular at a very popular Starwhats Coffeehouse just outside of the perimeter of metro Atlanta. This particular Starwhats offers several things daily: tepid coffee, mediocre pastries, polite conversation, and good chess.

The men, and few women, that gather to play chess at Starwhats range from people out for a walk that stumble in, to AUC Center students trying to escape campus life, to courtroom clerks done with work for the day, to civil servant retirees done with work forever. Kind people not searching for Bobby Fischer or chess immortality. Affable people searching for a good chat and a good game. Most days at Starwhats it's casual slow play with casual, caffeinated, people. Well, until Joe shows up.

Someone once described golf as, a good walk ruined. Chess with

Joe is a good conversation utterly and completely destroyed. That's if it can be called a conversation at all. Joe has the amazing ability to speak without pause or cessation. To talk without ever taking a breath or an interest in what you've got to say. No conversational quarter is offered or given with Joe. He's a man devoid of commas. The endless, resonant, Kenny G saxophone note of chat. Duotones Joe. It's quite the feat.

Also be forewarned, and wallow in the knowledge that if you've done anything of note in this thing we call life Joe has done it too. But better. If you've run a 5k in Boston, Joe has run a marathon on the moon. If you used to sing in the church choir, Joe gave Whitney Houston voice lessons. If you've recently read a good book, Joe has read all of the good books... yesterday. He's an omnipresent, insufferable, but tolerated part of the Starwhats Coffee chess community.

One day while pushing pawns and subjecting players to puffery about how the film *Love and Basketball* was inspired by his one-time romance with Sanaa Lathan, the scent of Yves Saint Laurent Eau De Toilette began to float through Starwhats like an old haint visiting new haunts. Then a voice, warm and commanding, rose over the hyperbole and asked,

"Have you ever played chess in Woodruff Park?"

No one knows how it was known, but everyone knew the question was intended for Joe. A hush fell over the packed room because everyone also knew where, and what, Woodruff Park was. Where Starwhats was the home of casual chess play, Woodruff Park was where the chess hustlers, and people with serrated edges to their lives and games played chess. Where Starwhats was filled with cool people

84

looking for a chill game, Woodruff Park was filled with rough and tumble folk playing for a dollar, playing for a meal, playing for shelter. In the jungle that is chess Woodruff Park was where the lions slept, dwelled, and pushed pawns.

All of the eyes in the coffee shop turned to Joe. None of them had ever played at Woodruff and for his many fantastic tales Joe had never mentioned playing there either. Joe felt the expectant stares of everyone in the suddenly eerily quiet coffee shop laser locked on him. He sat up straight, cleared his throat, and said,

"Of course. Of course! I used to play there before it was even called Woodruff Park!"

All eyes moved through the room searching for whoever had asked the question. Then from a different, distant, place in the crowded room the voice rose again.

"What was it called before it was *even* called Woodruff Park?"

Again, everyone turned to Joe. Joe looked like a contestant during final Jeopardy. The music and the clock are winding down and he has no idea what the right answer (question) is.

"Uhm … I uhm … I just called it Robert Park back then."

"Back in the early-eighties? Before anyone *even* knew Robert Woodruff was the benefactor you called it Robert Park? Curious."

The word curious was followed by the scent of YSL filling every corner of the room. It was like suddenly the voice, the man, his presence, was everywhere. Then, after a long fragrant silence, a man walked through the doors of the Starwhats with a copy of the *Atlanta Journal Constitution* tucked under his right arm.

"Curious," he said as he crossed the door sill, leaving no doubt that he was the source of the voice and the cologne. Hadn't he already been in the room? All eyes including Joe's fell upon him.

He was Frankie Beverly and Maze "Golden Time of Day," brown. An older gentleman donned in a suit from a time even older. A double breasted blood red blazer with ochre leather buttons. Tan trousers with creases so sharp he could shear a sheep just by walking past a pasture. Silver cufflinks adorned the wrists of a muted blue linen shirt that was buttoned all the way to the top. The shirt's collar flared and sat outside of, and atop, the jacket's lapels. He wore no necktie, and sported spats over brown leather brogues.

Joe's jaw tightened as his eyes squinted into dashes. He wasn't used to being challenged, at all, but especially not at Starwhats. This is where he was a king on a throne with no heir apparent. A ruler whose words and edicts were taken as fact and law. Who was this interloper, this peasant, this peon calling into question his questionable statements.

Joe raised his head high into the YSL and responded,

"SOME people knew Robert Woodruff was indeed the benny factor!"

The well-dressed man reached down and smoothed his trousers, careful not to cut his hands.

"And *You* were one of those SOMEones that knew that he was the … benny? Curious indeed. But anyway a lot has changed since it was *Robert Park*. So, when you think your game is up to it you should return." With that the well-dressed man spun on his heels and moved toward the exit.

"My game is always up to it!!" Joe shouted as he crossed the room toward the stranger's back.

The man stopped on a dime, quickly turned, and locked eyes with Joe. The man's eyes were as dark and mysterious as the waters of the Okefenokee, and they carried within them the authority and correction of a parent's stare. Joe froze in his tracks as if someone on the schoolyard had yelled, red light. A mouth that never searched for words fell mute beneath the man's glare. Joe's eyes, seemingly against their will, went to the floor. The well-dressed man took a full step forward. Joe's fingers began to pull at the seams of his jeans.

The man stood there just long enough for it to feel awkward to everyone, and said,

"Well then Joe, I look forward to seeing you in the park. Soon. Upon your arrival ask for Jihad."

With that he turned again and left. The door had just closed behind him when Joe found the nerve to look up. As all eyes in the coffeehouse seemed to once again be on Joe, he wondered how the man had known his name.

He pushed that thought aside, cleared his throat and in his full, newly found, voice shouted,

"Damn right you look forward!" to the closed door.

A week later, just after two in the afternoon on a Wednesday, Joe for the first time in his life walked into Woodruff Park.

Woodruff Park was no comfortable coffee shop just outside of Atlanta's perimeter. This was a small densely packed green space in the heart of the city. It was wild. It was brash. It was packed curb to clouds with people, sounds, and smells Joe was unaccustomed to. It seemed like Bedlam. Like a kingdom without a king. Like a nuthouse being run by the squirrels.

Everyone in the park seemed to speak as loud, or louder, than Joe. There were shouts followed by laughter. There was laughter followed by threats. People hugged each other in joy. People tussled with each other in anger. There were sirens and screams. There were tender touches and hard looks. He felt like a tourist in a world he didn't know. Didn't necessarily want to know.

He'd heard someone say in a movie once, "Upon entering the prison yard you should show no fear and immediately establish dominance." This wasn't a prison yard but it felt like what he imagined one would be.

Joe raised his head, cleared his throat, and said with as much confidence as he could muster,

"I'm looking for Jihad!"

His voice was drowned out by a car horn, mixed in with a crash of breaking glass, and carried away on a breeze with the sounds of the city. His exclamation had landed with the impact of a raindrop in the ocean. He felt his head begin to fall in defeat but instantly redoubled his resolve. He lifted his chin, squared his shoulders and said again, louder, "I'm looking for Jihad!!"

This time he caught the attention of LiLi. She was standing amongst friends and cohorts in short-shorts and leaned over Ugg boots that had seen better days and alleyways. She was thin. Too thin. Thin in that way that lets you know a person isn't well. Lili hadn't been well in some time. Throat cancer. Her skin was brown and ashen like she was wearing foundation made for White women by White men. She wasn't. Lili twisted and tugged at the bottom of a wrinkled tank top with the phrase, "Fck Wit It! " silk screened across the chest. She turned to face this new voice trying to find purchase in the park. She raised a lit cigarette up to her jugular notch, up to her trach tube, and took a pull. The smoke traveled down into her lungs, and back up her throat like salmon heading home. Lili looked over at Joe as smoke seeped from her trach tube and leaked through slightly parted lips like an angry dragon doing a magic trick. She shouted back over to him,

"You looking for Jihad? I'm looking for dick haaard!"

In what felt like practiced unison, what sounded like the entire park erupted into laughter. Joe felt himself shrinking in the moment.

He was searching for an appropriate response when he heard a voice with a calm and steady tone cut through the laughter and say,

"I'm the one you seek. I'm Jihad."

Joe turned toward the voice expecting to see the well-dressed man that visited Starwhats the week prior. Instead his eyes fell upon a Black man draped in a white thawb. Jihad sat with his hands in his lap and his back ironing board straight. He stared at Joe with the same swamp colored irises as the well-dressed man. In this man's eyes however lived a gentle weariness that seemed to run counter to the small cuts and deep scars that peppered his face. He looked young despite the injuries but his countenance testified to a hard life. He sported a full beard but no mustache. Beneath his thawb he wore cuffed blue jeans. On his feet Timberland boots. On his head a keffiyeh. Jihad sat at a table with a chessboard already carved into it. His chess pieces were in place and at the ready.

"You're Jihad?" Joe said, his arms flailing slightly.

"As I've said," came the flat reply.

"I see. I see. Well I was told I needed to come to the park and play you in a game of chess."

"Who would say such a thing to you?" Jihad said with unfeigned curiosity.

"An old dude that smelled like a whore and dressed like a pimp."

Jihad chuckled to himself and said under his breath,

"Pluto, you devil."

Joe, not hearing his reply said,

"What?"

Jihad laughed a bit louder, smiled a smile that didn't reach his eyes, and gestured to the seat across the table from him.

"Nothing. Please, sit. Let's play. Now I must tell you I play for five dollars. No less."

"Five dollars!?" Joe said, with his voice finding level and his arms beginning to flail wildly. Jihad sat as still as stagnant water, his gentle eyes hardening.

"No less. Do you still care to play?"

Joe contemplated the offer. Five dollars was no grand expense to him but he was unaccustomed to gambling on chess. Then he heard the well-dressed man's voice in his head, *when you think your game is up to it you should return.* This was followed by an actor's voice, *upon entering the prison yard you should show no fear and immediately establish dominance*. With these two thoughts caroming through his head he accepted the five dollar challenge but with a caveat.

"Okay. But let's play at that table!"

Joe pointed to a table a few feet away, and in the sun.

Jihad smirked, sucked his teeth, smiled, and replied,

"No thank you. I play here, or I play nowhere."

*Immediately establish dominance*. Raising his voice ever so slightly and flailing his arms all the more wildly Joe responded, "What are you talking about!? It's just over there. Stop being stupid."

Jihad smirked and sucked his teeth, but now a deep darkness had entered his eyes. It was the kind of darkness that moves over the land just as the wind picks up and a storm rolls in. It was the kind of darkness that hides within its velvety embrace a threat both immanent and apparent. It was the kind of darkness that most would heed, and avoid. From that kind of darkness came a voice menacing and firm.

"I play here. Or I play nowhere."

*Show no fear*. Joe doubled down.

"You're talking crazy! It's just over there!"

And with that Joe took his eyes off Jihad, off the darkness. Joe began picking Jihad's chess pieces with the intention of moving them to the table just a few feet away, in the sun.

Joe never saw Jihad stand. He missed the speed at which Jihad's right fist crossed the table. He caught not even a glimpse of Jihad's knuckles as they landed squarely against his left eye. The ground approached and reached him unseen. Joe crashed, unconscious, to the earth with the force of the asteroid that killed the dinosaurs. Jihad grabbed the chess pieces in Joe's limp hand, scooped the rest from the table into a satchel, and left the park with a speed that would have made one question if he'd ever been there at all.

Joe woke on the ground, in the sun, to the smell of a Newport being smoked via trach tube. He was welcomed back into consciousness by the sound of a voice shouting,

"You got knocked the fuck out!" followed by raucous laughter.

He doesn't remember how he got to his feet, or how he made it home, but he did. For three weeks he watched in the mirror as his eye went from purple and closed, to black and swollen, to almost brown and back to factory settings. A week after that, sporting an eye that still carried the remnants and a reminder of his visit to Woodruff, Joe sat in Starwhats once again a roaring charging lion amongst kittens.

Joe sat across the board from Mitch, one of the regulars. Mitch tried not to notice or mention Joe's eye but it was the injured elephant in the room. He adjusted the pieces on the board and in as benign of a tone as he could muster asked,

"So. What happened to your eye Joe?"

Joe felt everyone, again, staring at him.

"My eye? My eye!?" he said as his arms began to flail, "You should see the other guy's eye! I went down to Woodruff Park and beat those guys in chess so bad that three of them jumped me!"

No one said anything. The air was still. The statement sat there in the silence like a bull shit in a china shop. Then the scent of Yves Saint Laurent Eau De Toilette began to fill the room like an old haint visiting new haunts. Joe looked up and Mitch was no longer sitting across from him. It was now, somehow, the well-dressed older gentleman. Joe couldn't hide his surprise as the gentleman pushed pawn E4 and said,

"Three guys jumped you? Curious."

# Six Minutes

[a Club Quarantine Story || Fiction]

## Six Minutes
### [a Club Quarantine Story || Fiction]

I'll never forget it. Richmond Virginia, the summer of '89. The
smell of Phillip Morris cigarettes and What-A-Burger bologna would
hang heavy on the morning breeze. Beneath the noon day sun the
sidewalks and drug addicts both appeared broken and cracked. The
sounds of Hip Hop and Go-Go, "Warm it up, Kane" and "Run Joe,"
floated through the windows of Jetta GLIs and kitted out Escort GTs as
they rolled down streets that weren't paved with gold or taxpayer dollars.
Disney was flirting with the idea of putting a theme park in Manassas,
Gerald Baliles was still Governor, and my jump shot wasn't falling.
Little seemed right but everything felt possible.

We'd just graduated high school. We being Black Vince, Greggy
Greg, Candy and me, Ed. We called ourselves The Get Fresh Crew
because the song "The Show" by Doug E Fresh and Slick Rick was
everything to us. Those horns, those drums, Doug E on the beatbox, and
Slick Rick on the rap. If it wasn't perfect it was so close to perfection
that you could reach out and touch it. In well-lit school cafeteria dances,
and dimly lit nightclubs like The Ebony Island, we wopped so hard to
"The Show" that 'til this day I have issues with my neck and back. Every
time I get a new chiropractor I tell them up front that I have old wop
wounds from late 80s dance floor battles and linoleum breakdance wars.
They salute and thank me for my service. In '89 you couldn't have
convinced us that a better hip hop song would ever be made. Standing

here today in the year of our god (M.C.) 2020, it's possible that a better hip hop song never was.

We also earned our sobriquet, The Get Fresh Crew, because we were always trying to get fresh. We lived on a constant hunt for new jeans, sweatshirts, and sneakers. Especially sneakers. The shoes du jour were black and white (*Different Strokes)* shell toe Adidas with no laces, and two-toned (vitiligo) Diadoras with the fat laces. If you wanted to order off menu you could seek out the Wyoming white, Le Coq Sportif with the New Orleans black strap across the laces. Those were the top shelf kicks, but rest assured we coveted any and all fly sneaks. Especially the ones no one else had. The best feeling in the world was to walk up to the neighborhood playground, or down the high school hallways, in your crispy new sneakers, extend your foot like Cinderella trying to come up out of poverty and say, "Oh! Y'all ain't got these!" Or to look at someone else's BRAND NEW sneakers and say, "Those old! I been had those three months ago!"

If God made a better feeling than using bad grammar to insult new shoes he certainly kept it for himself. The only thing in life, at that time, remotely close to that feeling was getting the last Maple and Brown Sugar packet out of an oatmeal assorted flavors box. But be it securing fresh sneaks or winning the assorted oatmeal lotto The Get Fresh Crew rarely if ever got to experience the best feelings. We were broke-broke. So broke you had to say it twice. Our shoe shopping experience was more of the A&N, Thom McCann, bin in the middle of a grocery store aisle filled with nondescript shoes zip-tied together experience.

In junior high, once, in a red NowLatuh fueled, mind-addled search for the best feeling I drew a Nike symbol on the side of a pair of plain white canvas sneakers (a.k.a bobos) with a black Crayola marker. I wore those counterfeits to school, and figured that if I kept my feet in a state of perpetual motion no one would be able to notice. The whole day I looked like I had to desperately pee. My feet danced without ceasing like James Brown on the Night Train, or like Ned the wino on a different Night Train. By second period math I was sweating like a premenopausal woman on a relatively cool day. Halfway through third period English the teacher took me by the sweaty collar, escorted me to the school office, and told the principal that she suspected that I was on "the" crack. I finally had to confess that I was not on crack. I was on Crayola. That day in the school office, as the principal and English teacher debated if stupidity was a punishable offense, was the first time I met Black Vince. He was there because he'd punched the principal in the face.

Get Fresh was a motley crew. Black Vince was tall for a kid and had a slim build. He was called Black Vince by everyone, including us, to distinguish him from Bowlegged Vince and Stank Vince, and because he was very darkly complected. I mean with the naked eye you couldn't tell where his hairline stopped and his forehead began. He was dark at the worst time to be dark in the 80s, when Al B. Sure was in effect mode. This was before Wesley Snipes threatened to turn Christopher William's five dollar ass into change. Vince was so dark that most people joking on him would begin with, "You so black that..." and the infinite possible endings evolved from there.

"You so black that if I stabbed you right now I'd strike oil!"

97

"You so black that the pot calls the kettle, Vince!"

"You so black that Midnight strikes you!" and on and on and on.

Vince always smiled and laughed along good naturedly like, good one. However, if you looked into his eyes, and you didn't have to look deep, you could tell he was hurt by the constant ribbing. A school full of Black kids making fun of him for being black. For being considered too much of what we all were. How could it not hurt? All of the jokes and negative comments created within him an ever growing insecurity. He became a guy always trying to fit in, impress people, and curry favor. In this pursuit he'd do just about anything he was dared to do.

He was once dared to punch the principal in the face. He did it. Also, his father was the principal of the school at the time. He was suspended from school, and damn near suspended from home as well. At his core, Vince was a nice guy. He was easily influenced into bad choices and struggled to be liked, but he was a nice guy all the same. Not everyone could say that.

Greggy Grey couldn't. Greg was loved, and Greg was crazy. Girl crazy mostly. As luck would have it girls were crazy about him too so that was convenient. During the late 80s reign of Al B. Sure, first of his name, Greg kind of looked like Al B. Sure. If you tilted your head to the side and squinted a little bit they could have passed for fourth cousins twice removed. One of the differences between Greg and Al B was that Greg had two eyebrows. Another was that Al had curly hair and Greg's hair was wavy. 2B or not 2B that was the question. The most striking difference between the crooner and the Get Fresh Crew member was that

Greg had grown up with a fairly bad stutter. His struggle to get his words out, and propensity to repeat himself while attempting to do so, was how he earned the nickname Greggy Greg. In elementary school, after class, he met with a speech therapist every day, worked hard, and eventually overcame his stutter. By high school it only showed up when he was mad or nervous, and he was rarely nervous.

The teasing about his stutter left him angry. That anger slept just below the surface, and when it did wake it seemed to often be taken out on girls. Girls seemed to forgive him his anger because of his good looks, and his good looks afforded him unfettered access to just about any girl. Back then it seemed like any girl I liked, liked Greg, and Greg liked any girl that liked him. This made the relationship between Greg and myself less than ideal.

The only girl in The Get Fresh Crew was Candy. What no one knew, including Candy, was that she and I were meant to be together. Songs like, "Candy Girl" by New Edition, "Kanday" by LL Cool J, and "Candy" by Cameo had made it clear. I mean Larry Blackmon, James Todd Smith, and Ralph Tresvant wouldn't lie to me, to her, to us. Would they? No, of course not. All of the RnB, funk, and hip hop signs portended to the provenance and destiny of our union.

The issue with liking Candy was that I couldn't let Greg, or Candy, know that I liked her. If I expressed interest in Candy, it seemed assured that she'd tell me that she was interested in Greg. Greg, of course, would then have no choice but to start showing interest in her. Then they'd date and end up making a fool of Larry Blackmon, James

Todd Smith, and Ralph Tresvant. So in order to have a chance with her, and to save the prognostic integrity of music, I had to express no interest in her and thus secure her affections via my almost complete silence and abject distance. It seemed to make sense at the time. Did I mention that I was young?

One afternoon in the summer of '89 I was walking past Candy's house as she sat on her front porch listening to the radio and rapping along with "The Show." After Doug E had confessed that his shoes were ill fit and caused injury to his corns, at the top of her lungs Candy rapped, "Six minutes, six minutes, six minutes and I'm fresh, you're on!"

*And I'm fresh you're on?* I stopped dead in my tracks. No. There's no way she thought that was the lyric. We loved that song too much not to know its every word and beat break. It was clearly, certainly, just a slip of the tongue, a mix up in the mind, or perhaps I'd just heard it wrong. Yes. That's what it was. That's what it had to be. I'd heard it wrong. Just then the radio DJ did a backspin on the record and brought that section back. Candy again shouted at the top of her lungs,

"Six minutes, six minutes, six minutes and I'm fresh, you're on!"

Jesus Christ! It was sacrilege I tell you. Our god MC who art in Harlem would have rejected this burnt lyrical offering and visited upon us a plague of seven wack rappers. What was I to do? Could anything be done? I said to myself, just let it go, just keep on walking. Instead I slowly turned my head, like a Black Chucky doll, looked at her and said, "... That's not how it goes."

Why! Why had I done that!? She turned off the radio, looked at

100

me like a pair of bobos with a Nike symbol draw on the side in black marker, and replied, "What!? Yeah-huh it does!"

I looked at her like she was the most beautiful thing my eighteen year old eyes had ever seen and said, "Yeah. Nah."

She stood, crossed her arms across her chest, rolled her neck and said, "Then what it say then stupid boy!"

I turned completely and faced her. I felt like I was looking directly into the sun. I took a deep breath and replied, "It says six minutes, six minutes, six minutes, Doug E Fresh, you're on. Uh-uh-on."

She stared at me for a second, then looked up at the sky as if replaying the song in her head with these new apocryphal lyrics, and said, "So! My name ain't Doug E! So I'm going to keep singing it my way!"

"Cool," I replied.

I forced myself to stop looking at her, but just like anyone that's stared at the sun her image still glowed on my retinas. I turned and as I began to walk away she interjected, "But thanks for telling me. Everybody else just let me be out here loud, wrong, and not knowing. I mean I'm still going to be loud and wrong, but at least I know."

She laughed. I didn't. I turned fully toward her again. I stood there trying to figure out how to put this tangled ball of yarn that doubled as my feelings into words. I tugged at the strings, pulled at the edges, but couldn't unravel it. My eyes began to water with frustration. Then her eyes, eyes that always seemed to be dissecting, dismembering and looking for a joke, softened. It was like she could see, and feel, the struggle in me. Like she could sense the part of me drowning in my own feelings. The part of me kicking hard in an effort to break the surface. The part of me red rovering in the hopes that words would come over. They didn't.

I blinked the tears away and again said, "... Cool."

I walked away feeling defeated, and never looked back.

Summer ended, fall descended, and The Get Fresh Crew went our separate ways. I went to college in the Shenandoah Valley and studied business. That September someone dared Black Vince to sell a dime of weed, which turned into a quarter, then an ounce of coke, then a pound, then a key. It was the key that he got caught with. I always thought it ironic that they called it a key. It never seemed to open the right doors. Greggy-Greg got Rhonda Kenton pregnant. I heard they married, had a son, and divorced soon after with her citing spousal abuse. Candy went to a school near D.C. We exchanged a few letters but lost touch completely by our sophomore year.

Once while flipping through my high school yearbook with my girlfriend at the time, I told her about The Get Fresh Crew. How close we were. How I hadn't seen or heard from them in years. She asked, what happened to you guys? I told her ... life happened.

I once read somewhere that life can be like a mighty river. Like the Mississippi. Unstoppable, with bends and twists, but flowing ever forward. It read

*One's life may split from the mainstream, cut its own path, and*

*seek its own level. Or it may be more like a tributary that meanders until it finds a way to connect to something greater, some more expansive, something going somewhere you've never been. But no matter what, through time, terrain, rain and drought, mighty rivers, and life, keep moving.* Yeah. I read somewhere that life can be like the mighty Mississippi and we are but driftwood following the flow, lost and found in the stream, caught in the current.

My twenties came with advanced degrees, a career, a house, a car, a girlfriend turned wife, and kids. My thirties came with promotions, a divorce, an apartment, and seeing my kids on the weekends. My forties have thus far come with a mid-life crisis, a therapist, a career change, and Tinder. Life has not turned out to be the white picket fence wrapped around the corner lot house that I imagined it would be. No, my imaginary house burned to the ground and a tornado ran away with the fence. I have vowed to rebuild but haven't managed to pick up a hammer just yet.

Tonight as I sit in my apartment staring at a microwave dinner and wondering if this can even be considered food, I get a text from a friend from work. Mark.

(M) 10:00 PM: *Yo! You on IG? D-Nice's Live is going crazy! He's spinning nothing but everything! And everybody in here! Log in bruh!*

I hate being called bruh.

Mark is just north of fifty but desperately wants to be twenty two. This is apparent by the general snugness of his jeans, his insistence on calling me his slime (whatever that means), and his obsession with posting Tik Tok videos of him doing dances he cannot (and should not) do. But as aggravating as he can sometimes be it would actually be good to see him today. I haven't seen Mark, or almost anyone, in a week. COVID-19, a respiratory viral infection with no known cure, in short order ran roughshod across the world a month ago. The entire nation was swiftly swept up, like driftwood, and deposited into our homes. In some states, people were asked to shelter in place. In certain counties, communities were instructed to stay at home. In the city of Atlanta, folk were told to sit yo asses down and chill out. All of this was in an effort to give the government enough time to figure out how to save the economy. And us.

They call it social distancing but it feels like complete isolation. Like I'm stuck in a prison that I've built myself, and as it turns out I'm not a quality contractor. I've told myself that when this is over I HAVE to put some better paint on these prison walls. My kids are with my ex-wife. We Skype every night, but other than that it's just me and my thoughts.

So, I take Mark's advice and log into IG under my username, EdEddnEddy. I swim into the stream of D-Nice's Live, And holy shit! the whole world IS in here! There are seventy-five thousand people from a little bit of everywhere listening to D-Nice spin records. If they have wifi in hell I'm sure Satan is logged in and in the chat requesting "Hot in Here" by Nelly. Tiffany Haddish just told Common to stop virtually touching her butt. Spice Adams just did a dance, via split screen, in a leisure suit that appears to be made from curtains my great grandma

104

threw out in the fifties. Someone said that Oprah is buying out the imaginary bar. What kind of musical, virtual, sorcery is this?

D-Nice stands between a set of turntables and an ever purpling skyline. He's wearing a wide brimmed hat, a t-shirt, and blue jeans. He's spinning "Lady Marmalade" to an enrapt, excited, and grateful audience of listeners. Myself included. He's playing comfort music for a nation that needs something to tamp down the fear that's been knocking at the back of our collective skulls for weeks.

"We got Patti LaBelle in here y'all! Patti LaBelle!" D-Nice shouts as he changes hats.

His excitement is clear. The comment section of his Live fills with flower emojis, and people praising Ms. LaBelle. She returns the love by posting praying hands and heart emojis of her own. I'm tapping my foot and singing along to the music. I pull up the chat and type,

@EdEddnEddy

*Getchy getchy- yi-yi-yiyi!* -1m

I'm not concerned with spelling because how the hell is that actually spelled anyway?

Within seconds my message flows up, away, and disappears into the constant stream of comments. Comments tossed into the chat begin to feel like coins flipped into a fountain. Like wishes, hopes, and dreams. Sometimes like tearful prayers.

"Lady Marmalade" is followed by Aretha Franklin's "Rock Steady." The chat fills with halos, hearts, and R.I.P.'s.

"Everybody post a goat right now! Post a goat for Aretha Franklin, one of the greatest of all time. May she rest in peace!" D-Nice shouts.

As if having been instructed by Simon of Simon Says fame, goat emojis begin to dominate and graze through the chat.

I'm looking at the usernames that accompany the fast moving, disappearing, never to be seen again comments. There are people I work with, went to college with, and that owe me money listening. I imagine them in their homes singing along to hits old and new. I see the names of people that I've borrowed things from (and never returned) commenting. I imagine them in the glow of their laptop screens dancing to the music of our youth. It's all love, forgiveness, and reminiscing. The threat of death and dying has a way of bringing into sharp relief what really matters, and what really doesn't.

Then I see it briefly in the comment stream. It goes by so fast I almost miss it but then it appears again. Username: @TastesLikeCandyGirlRVA89. No, it couldn't be.

"We got 80 thousand people! 80 thousand rocking with us right now! And we got Slick Rick in here y'all! MC Ricky D in the place to be! You know I got to play something for the ruler!"

D-Nice says this with great respect and reverence like a believer staring at the face of his god MC as it emerges from a lightning filled word cloud. And then the horns blare! The drums drop! I look at the chat and

@TastesLikeCandyGirlRVA89

*Six minutes, six minutes, six minutes and I'm fresh, you're on!*

-1m

My heart stops and starts again. It's beating like it's, like I'm, eighteen years old. I look at the screen, stand, and begin walking in a circle with my hands over my mouth. Which is something we've been advised by the CDC not to do. The CDC says to reduce the risk of contracting COVID-19 refrain from touching your face. This announcement was made on national TV as the spokesperson giving the advice kept rubbing her eyes. So clearly it's meant to be taken with a grain of salt, and a mRNA shot.

I stop wearing out the hardwood floors and grab the tablet from my briefcase. I log into IG on the tablet and type @TastesLikeCandyGirlRVA89 into the search. The screen refreshes. A profile picture comes up and ... it's her. The proverbial one that got away. Candy.

I think back on simpler times, when the air was rife with bologna and tobacco. The days when we had more of life ahead of us than behind us. Our lives before bills and pills and mortgages and car notes. Summers not spent shackled in debt, or paying a debt to society in shackles. When we were all free but just didn't know it. Back when I felt like I could say anything to anyone except her. I think to who I was back then, and who I imagined I'd be today. I wonder if the me I used to be would be proud of the me I am. Tears begin to well in my eyes. I blink them away. I click on message and I'm typing before I know what I want to say.

@EdEddnEddy

*Candy! It's me! It's Ed! Ed from The Get Fresh Crew!* -1m

I hit send, stand, and begin wearing out the hardwood again. D-Nice has started spinning one of my favorite songs, "Soul Makossa" by Manu Dibango. My toe is tapping but not with the beat, with anticipation. My screen brightens and I see three undulating dots beneath my message. Oh shit! She got it! She's typing!

@TastesLikeCandyGirlRVA89

*Edwin!! OMG!* -1m

Other than my parents she's the only person that I have ever allowed to call me Edwin. A lump grows in my throat. No longer able, or wanting to hold them back, I type my response through tears

@EdEddnEddy

*Yes! Yes! Candy I can't*

*believe this!* -1m

@TastesLikeCandyGirlRVA89

*Right!* -2m

@EdEddnEddy

*I lost track of you after*

108

*college. -3m*

*@TastesLikeCandyGirlRVA89*

*I lost track of you during college!
-4m*

@EdEddnEddy

*True true true! -5m*

*@TastesLikeCandyGirlRVA89*

*Wow Edwin! This is crazy. Wow!
-6m*

@EdEddnEddy

*I saw your post in Club
Quarantine! I saw the
name and was like, nah!
So I looked up your
profile. -8m*

*@TastesLikeCandyGirlRVA89*

*Awww! That's the most precious
story of stalking I've ever heard!
-9m*

@EdEddnEddy

*Ahhh I see you still got jokes!*

*AND I looked at your profile*

*picture. You look the same!*

*-10m*

@TastesLikeCandyGirlRVA89

*I see your eyesight has really taken a beating over the years Edwin. But thank you! -11m*

@EdEddnEddy

*HAHAHA no really. -12m*

@TastesLikeCandyGirlRVA89

*Well your distinguished grays have come in very nicely sir. -13m*

@EdEddnEddy

*Ahh! Some co-stalking!*

*That's what took you*

*so long to reply? -14m*

@TastesLikeCandyGirlRVA89

*Well you know what EPMD said,*

*stalk me and I'll stalk you back.*

*-15m*

@EdEddnEddy

*That's not how that goes!*

*And my grays have come*

*in light but the pizzas have*

*come in heavy over the years*

*hahaha! -17m*

@TastesLikeCandyGirlRVA89

*Listen chile I understand! The other*
*day just to get out of the house I*
*took a walk around the block and*
*almost died! We are not in the*
*shape, and do not have the*
*metabolism, of teenagers anymore.*
*I watched a Pizza Hut commercial*
*yesterday and felt the cellulite grow*
*in my left thigh. My right thigh is*
*still super fine though! -19m*

@EdEddnEddy

*Still hilarious! How are*

*doing with this*

*quarantine? -20*m

@TastesLikeCandyGirlRVA89

*I'm doing. That's all anyone can do, just*
*be still, be prayerful, be careful, and hope*
*you see the people you love on the other*
*side of this madness. -22*m

@EdEddnEddy

*Yeah. Yeah, I feel that.*

*-23*m

@TastesLikeCandyGirlRVA89

*Listen Edwin, lets cut the bull! Let's*
*address the elephant in the chat room.*
*-24*m

My heart catches on the lump in my throat. What elephant in the room? Why are their elephants in rooms? I'm a speechless kid again looking for his, hiding and seeking, words. Like that kid I can only muster

@EdEddnEddy

*Cool.* -27m

@TastesLikeCandyGirlRVA89

*When you read it, did you correct
my six minutes post to read 'Doug
E Fresh' instead of 'And I'm fresh,'
like you did that day I was sitting
on my porch!? LOL* -29m

A sigh of relief, that no one can hear, escapes my lips. It's amazing that she can still take my breath away, and that she remembers that day.

@EdEddnEddy

*Of course I did! HAHAHA*

-30m

@TastesLikeCandyGirlRVA89

*I knew it!* -31m

At the bottom of my screen a news alert pops up.

***MSNBB: Breaking News: CDC estimates COVID-19 related deaths to top 375,000 in 2020.***

The threat of death and dying has a way of bringing into sharp relief what really matters, and what really doesn't. More than ever it feels like things not given voice might go unsaid forever. More than ever it feels like now or never. So I type.

@EdEddnEddy

*What you never knew was*

*how I felt about you when we*

*were kids. How my 18 year*

*old heart beat a little louder*

*when you were around. How*

*I stood a little taller when*

*you entered the room. How I*

*listened more closely whenever*

*you spoke. Yes, I corrected your*

*six minutes post but what I*

*really want to correct is the*

*record. -35m*

I type all of that, read it twice, and then reach for the backspace bar to erase it. A weird thing happens on my way to the backspace bar. I accidentally hit send. I think it was an accident. I don't know. Accident or not, I hit send and I wait.

It. Is. An eternity before those three dots began to blink again.

@TastesLikeCandyGirlRVA89

*Ed, why are you saying this now?*

*Tonight? -40m*

@EdEddnEddy

*Who knows if there will be*

*another tonight Candy. I've*

*not said things for too long.*

*I've missed out on promotions*

*because I didn't speak up. My*

*ex-wife and I were miserable*

*roommates just passing each*

*other on the stairs for about*

*five years before we could say*

*it. The time for saying things*

*is now, and so tonight it is.*

*Tonight it's 1989 and I'm*

*finally speaking my mind.*

*-44m*

I hit send and wait a full six minutes. Nothing. I stand and begin to circle again, again. Just as I am about to clarify myself, to let her know

115

that I have no expectations, that I just wanted to say the things I've wanted to say since I was fourteen, she replies,

@TastesLikeCandyGirlRVA89

*Ed, I married Greg. After he divorced Rhonda Kenton. We got married. -50m*

The color drains from my face. I feel light headed. Greggy-Greg. Pretty Muthahfuckah! Fuck him and the Shemar Moore he rode in on! Where is Nino Brown when really you need him! I never even told her I liked her, and still, there he was. I might as well have said it. Have shown it. I spent all that time being bullied into silence by, myself! I was my own Gooch. I should have...

@TastesLikeCandyGirlRVA89

*We're divorced now. We were married for five and have been divorced for almost eight. -1h*

I take a deep breath and only then realize that I'd been holding it. Typing, "Forget Greg, texturizers, Rick Fox, and Boris Kodjoe," seems inappropriate. So instead I go with,

@EdEddnEddy

*I'm sorry to hear that. -1h2m*

@TastesLikeCandyGirlRVA89

*No you're not!!! LOLOL* -1h3m


@EdEddnEddy

*You're right I'm not! HAHAHA*

*—1h4m*


@EdEddnEddy

*I mean, I am sorry to hear you
had to go through a divorce.
I've been through one and they
are hard, no matter what.* -1h5m


@TastesLikeCandyGirlRVA89

*Very true. Very true.* -1h6m

@EdEddnEddy

*I'm not sorry about you being
divorced from Greg though!
HAHAHA!* -1h7m

@TastesLikeCandyGirlRVA89

*Me neither! Pretty Muthahfuckah!*

-1h8m

@EdEddnEddy

*Listen! D-Nice has built us a*

*time machine and it may*

*only exist for one night.*

*I've got a Cabbage Patch*

*and a Roger Rabbit that I've*

*been saving for 30 years.*

*May I have this dance?*

-1h10m

@TastesLikeCandyGirlRVA89

*Under one condition. The*
*Strawberry Hill Boone's Farm is on*
*you! -1h11m*

@EdEddnEddy

*Deal! Strawberry Hills*

*forever! HAHAHA -1h12m*

118

I laugh and turn up the music. D-Nice is playing "Everything She Wants," by Wham. I receive a file in my inbox. It's a GIF of Candy doing The Prep. I laugh and send her one of me doing The Smurf. We exchange GIFs and emojis for the next few hours as the clock ticks forward and time turns back.

Around 1 a.m. my knees call it quits, and Candy texts that she's turning in for the night too. I get my last message of the evening from her.

@TastesLikeCandyGirlRVA89

*I needed this, Edwin. I needed this and didn't know it. Here's what I haven't said. I liked you all those years ago too, but thought that because you didn't talk to me, and seemed to be actively ignoring me, that you disliked me. Neither of us knew how to use our words back then but thank God we're grown now. So when this quarantine is over, and if your mama will let you come out and play, let's get a cup of coffee. Okay? It's still on you though!! LOLOL. I'll be looking for you in Club Quarantine tomorrow*

I stare at her message, smiling, and admiring the fact that she spelled Questlove with the question mark.

Earlier I remarked that I'd read that life can be like the mighty Mississippi, flowing forward with inevitability and certainty. That it may split into tributaries, or fork off like branches, but always it moves forward. Well, I also saw in a documentary that in 1812, due to an earthquake, The Mississippi River for several hours ran backward. The mighty, immutable, force of nature that is the Mississippi River ran backward.

Turns out that sometimes something can come along that shakes up everything. Something that will allow time, and the driftwood caught in its current, to flow back so that we might find things we lost along the way. And say the things we needed to say.

@EdEddnEddy

*Six minutes, six minutes, six*
*minutes and I'm fresh. I'm*
*gone.* - 3h9m

# *BLACC KOFFEE: A Pop-Up*

*[Fiction]*

# BLACC KOFFEE: A Pop-Up
## [Fiction]

1.

It appeared out of nowhere, like a wavy lush green oasis across an arid beige ancient desert. And like a sun-battered man crossing that desert, his dehydrated tongue stuck to the roof of his mouth, I suddenly felt gripped with an insatiable thirst and an unrelenting desire to quench it. I don't remember feeling even slightly parched before seeing it, but having seen it I was now gripped with desire, want, and need. The sign in front of the cart read, *BLACC KOFFEE: A Pop-Up*. I guess that's why they call them pop-ups, they appear out of nowhere.

There was a Black woman. Black? African American? To be honest I don't really see color. There was a woman standing on the other side of the cart chewing a piece of gum with the intensity of Violet Beauregarde approaching the third course. Her hair was doing something amazing, gravity defying, cultural. As a White man I know I'm not supposed to touch her hair. I've seen enough Tik-Tok videos to know that. That's a no-no. It'll get you canceled, doxed, and placed in eternal viral video hell. I'm not supposed to even want to touch her hair, but I do want to. I center my ally-ship, review my pronouns, check my privilege, and walk up. There's no line so in a few short steps I'm face to face with, Olo-Dumara. That's what her name tag reads. I wouldn't even begin to try to pronounce it... or touch her hair.

Her cheeks fill with air like Louis Armstrong standing center stage beneath the bright lights of Preservation Hall. Her lungs empty as she blows an impossibly large white bubble with her gum. For a moment it's all I can see. My world goes white, and there appears to be an oval? A football? no, an eye at the center of the bubble. Staring at me. It blinks. I blink and the bubble is gone as if it never existed. Had it existed?

Olo-Dumara smiles at me, her teeth as white and as wide as the bubble, real or imagined, had been. In her hand she holds a to-go paper cup of hot coffee. *Had it always been in her hand?* is what I think as the steam swirls and rises like morning fog in the light of a new day. The rich scent of the coffee swims the distance between Olo-Dumara and myself, and I'm drowned in how bold, sweet, floral, and strong it smells. I step closer, close my eyes, and lean over the cup so that I can smell the coffee more fully and feel its warmth wash over my face. I open my eyes and the cup is in my hand, warm and inviting. Instinctively I lift it to drink. From the back of Olo-Dumara's throat comes a loud and commanding click. It's a sound I've never heard before. Like God dancing to a Lil Jon song. Like the universe getting a back adjustment. It's a sound that demands my full attention. I look at her and she points to a sign on her left that reads, *Blacc Koffee is an immersive experience. Don't drink Blacc Koffee if you're allergic to immersive Koffee, or the Blacc experience. Nod if you accept.* Olo-Dumara stares at me, her eyes unblinking. Her ever-present smile is gone. I meet her gaze, and nod. She blinks, smiles, and I greedily drink the coffee.

Olo-Dumara watches me as I gulp down the cup. Her jaw

clinches and releases as she passionately chews her gum. I finish the cup, and in her hands she holds two bags of coffee beans. I wipe my mouth with the back of my hand and ask her if that's what I just drank. She nods and winks. I ask what the coffee is called so that I can order it the next time I visit. She nods toward a sign on her right that reads, *Koffee Will Make You Black Blend: One Cup and Two Bags Free: Guaranteed to Change Your Life*. I ask, so it's free then? She winks with her other eye and extends the two bags of coffee to me. As I reach for them her cheeks begin to fill like Dizzy Gillespie preparing to cut heads at Minton's Playhouse. A small white bubble pushes from between her lips. Her cheeks sink in as the bubble fills and grows between us. I reach for the bags and in doing so my nose touches the tip of the bubble. The bubble bursts, I blink, and she's gone. I stand alone on the sidewalk looking for Olo-Dumara. Searching for the coffee stand. Neither are to be found. I guess that's why they call it a pop-up. The only evidence that either were there are the two bags of coffee in my hand. I stand there in my tan khakis, brown loafers, powder blue shirt and navy blue sweater thinking, I wish I'd have touched her hair.

2.

I always wear a small crossbody bag when I walk in the city. I found it using Bing so I nicknamed it Bing Cross-B. Absolutely no one born after 1960 finds this remotely humorous. I keep my wallet and my keys in the bag but it has plenty of room. Not to mention it's comfortable and discourages theft. The other day some idiot shouted, nice purse! It's not a purse. It's a small crossbody bag for men. I don't know why that's so hard for people to understand. Prince, the artist and the artist formerly known as, wore shoes with high heels but were they high heeled shoes? No. They were shoes with high heels for men. Seems clear. I put the two bags of coffee in Bing Cross-B for men and continue my walk to work. I look at my watch. It's nine on the head. Surprisingly my coffee pitstop doesn't seem to have put me behind even a second. Which is good because there are lots of people downtown today. Looks like a protest or something is happening.

As I walk into my office building just off Woodruff Park one of my co-workers, Brian, is walking out. I wave but he doesn't see me. Or maybe he does; he's a strange one. I scan my access badge and Bridgette, one of the many rotating armed guards in the lobby, says, "Nice tan." She taps the grip of her gun lightly with her index finger and winks at me while chewing gum. Olo-Dumara? No. Bridgette's worked here as long as I have. This, however, has never happened before and I have no idea what it means. Is she flirting with me? Is she threatening me? Is she threatening to flirt with me or flirting with threatening me? I pull my crossbody bag closer across my body, and step onto the elevator. As the door is closing I hear her shout, "Nice purse."

It's not.

A muzak version of Michael Jackson's, "Man in the Mirror" begins playing just as the doors ease shut. The elevator is mirrored. The walls, the ceiling, every surface except the floor (for HR reasons) is reflective. I catch a glimpse of my own visage and have to put my hand to my face to ensure it's me. I walk toward the mirror, my mouth agape. Bridgette was right. I have tanned. My complexion makes me look almost Latin. North of Ricardo Montalban but south of Erik Estrada. Geraldo Rivera if you will. My skin is tan and smooth. My hair looks longer. Have I not been paying attention? Today was a bit brisk but the sun was definitely out and beaming. Global warming hasn't gone this far? It hasn't become global tanning has it? Every day I wake early, brush my teeth, shower, and dress without ever really looking in the mirror. Maybe I've been this brown for weeks. I did go down to New Orleans last month. Maybe it was all that time in the sun with no hat on Bourbon Street or Tchoupitoulas. The elevator stops and the doors open.

I walk off of the elevator backward, gobsmacked that the image receding in the mirror is me. The doors close and I turn around. My boss stands up and looks over the top of his cubicle. He immediately spots me. He looks from me to Bing Cross-B, and comes out of his cubicle in a huff. I look at my watch. I'm not late. Actually I'm ten minutes early. He's approaching with deliberate speed. I find myself walking back a bit. He's about four steps away when he begins pointing at my bag and shouting, "I told you guys last week, messengers use the service elevators!"

I look around, confused.

He says, "Yeah you!"

I say, "Ryan?" We're almost nose to nose when he stops. It's as if the sound of my voice has freed him from a trance. He looks like someone has thrown a bucket of cold water in his face. His brow smooths. His hackles settle.

He squints and stares at me trying to reconcile the voice and the face. Then he says, "Gavin?"

I say, "Yes!"

He laughs and says, "My God man."

I say, "I'm not anyone's God."

He laughs again and says, "Overuse of tanning beds can increase squamous cell carcinoma by fifty-eight percent and basal cell carcinoma by twenty four percent. That's a fact. Keep it in mind." He slaps me on the back and walks away still laughing.

Heads pop up over the tops of the cubicles like Whack-a-moles. I hear the voices of my coworkers whispering, "Everybody wants to be Black but nobody wants to be Black."

"He's kind of cute."

"No way he's getting another promotion now."

"He must have started dating on the southside."

"Gavin done turned into Geraldo."

I knew it! Geraldo Rivera. I retreat to the all accepting, come as you are, What Would Jesus Poo, gender neutral restroom. I feel odd. I feel different. I duck into the handicapped stall, close and lock the door just as a muzak version of Aretha Franklin's, "Natural Woman," begins to play.

3.

I used to have bouts of anxiety when I was young. Fear really. Nothing as simple as a knock in the attic or a bump in the night. No. I think I was ten years old when my uncle first started telling me about how my future was in jeopardy because the Blacks were stealing my jobs. I thought, the Blacks are stealing paper routes? This sounded odd but my uncle seemed like a learned man. A man of letters. Those letters were often NSF, but they were letters all the same. Then around twelve he told me that the Blacks were lazy, it was actually the Mexicans who were now stealing my jobs. I thought, the Mexicans are going to start taking out the trash, pulling up their grade in science, stop being mean to my sister, and therefore gain access to my allowance? If they were willing to do it, especially the sister part, then maybe they deserved the weekly twenty dollars that I wasn't getting because I'd done none of it. I think I was sixteen when I was informed that the Blacks and the Mexicans had taken a lazy back seat to all women. All women were stealing my jobs. At that time in my life you'd have thought my employment was hands-on, and the position required Jergens lotion, Kleenex tissue 3-ply ultra soft, a strong wifi signal, and a locked bathroom door. A door locked just like the one to the bathroom stall I currently find myself taking deep breaths in.

For the record I don't recommend taking deep breaths in a public restroom. The air tastes like poor dietary decisions, and smells like it tastes. I ignore the assault on two fifths of my senses and lean back heavily against the stall door. In my head I see Hodor from Game of Thrones fulfilling his seizure promised destiny. I spread my arms against

128

the door of the stall, as if holding back an army of White Walkers, and say aloud to no one, "Hodor!" I chuckle to myself. The moment of levity helps me to slow my breathing and taste less of the air. I use my shirt sleeve to wipe away the beads of sweat that have begun to polka dot my forehead.

I don't know if it's the nerves or the coffee but suddenly I have to pee like a drunk man at his front door at 3 a.m. fumbling with his keys. I unzip my pants, reach in and, nothing. My hand searches and key fumbles about, but there's nothing there. Nothing. I hurriedly drop my pants and my briefs, and slowly, nervously, look down. My uncle was right, a woman has taken my job. A Black woman at that.


4.

What in the entire Black Lives Matter, Say Her Name, fuck is going on! I still have to pee, badly, maybe even worse now, but I don't have the usual equipment. I feel myself about to air spray the walls so I flop down on the toilet seat. All of the surfaces in the stall are stainless steel and reflective, except the floor (not for HR reasons). As I begin to relieve myself the face staring back at me, its jaw open in horror and amazement, is not my own. Not in color, gender, shape, or form. It's the face that tucks little White kids in at night and tells them they is smart, they is kind, and they is important in academy award winning films. It's the face of the eternally single, perpetually sassy, slightly overweight best friend with all the great comebacks in rom-coms. It's the face of the girl I slept with in college out of curiosity and denied ever knowing the next day. It's the last face my uncle warned me about. I know I've seen it somewhere before.

My nervous bladder completely empties itself. Which is a relief but I'm immediately confronted with the age old question of, which way to wipe. I've never owned a vagina? vulva? uterus? One of these! All of these? I barely know what they're called much less how they work! I've heard that wiping the wrong way will give you crabs, syphilis, a UTI and cause your ass to itch. Landing on the proper approach is fifty-fifty so I wipe back to front, flush the toilet, pull up my pants, and hope that I have good health insurance just in case whatever is happening to me is permanent.

I stumble out of the stall and to the mirror, my hands against my face. I immediately realize I should have washed my hands first but it's too late. I stare at my hair. My compromised hands inch from my cheeks, to my brow, and stop short. My hands tremble. Is this my hair? Can I touch it now? Before I can answer the question, or tangle my fingers in the mirror's mane, the bathroom door swings open. Mindy and Elizabeth walk in. They're all laughs until they see me, covered in sweat, looking at them in confused horror.

Mindy, Elizabeth, and I have worked here for almost the same amount of time. We started within weeks of each other. Mindy is an Irish Catholic White woman from Long Island that talks like Fran Drescher and Snooki had a baby and only ever let that baby watch movies starring Marisa Tomei. Elizabeth is Mexican, from Salma Hayek Veracruz Mexico, but for all intents and purposes, she's a White woman. Her accent only surfaces when she's angry. Other than that she sounds, and with a little makeup looks, like Katie Couric. Which is the desired look.

They look at me, then each other, then at me, smile, join hands like the twins in *The Shining*, and begin slowly walking toward me. And somehow I know it's coming. I've been a Black woman for less than five minutes and I feel it coming in my less than five minutes old Black bones. Mindy and Elizabeth reach out with their free hands, and say in unison, "Can I touch your hair?"

5.

I step back avoiding and evading their 4c hungry hands. 4c? How do I know my hair is 4c? Is it 4c? What the hell even is 4c!? Not only do I somehow know this, I'm also acutely aware that I now know how to double dutch, how to do a line dance to a song by someone named Tamia, that I should only buy the hair grease in the green jar, and that I feel strongly that Jiffy ain't cornbread. It's not? I am becoming a revelation unto myself, a diary written by a new me being read by the old. Before I can dig into what, if any, other new knowledge has been bestowed upon me I see that Mindy and Elizabeth have closed the distance between us. Their hands desperate for Black tresses, African American manes, Negro locs, are stretching, straining, and almost all up in my kitchen. How dare they! I haven't even touched whoever's hair this is!

I reach down within myself and in a voice that is north of *Diary of a Mad Black Woman*, Madea, and south of *That's My Mama*, Theresa

Merritt, (Diahann Carroll in *Claudine* firm if you will) I say, "NO!" I don't just say it, I mean it. With my feet planted, arms akimbo, and hands on newly found hips, I embody it. Mindy and Elizabeth don't just stop, they freeze.

I'm not sure if a firm, Black woman, No, harkens them back to a nonsense mammy nanny from their past, or if it's just a word they've never heard before from a black anything or a Black anyone. Whatever the reason they stand frozen like the Tin Man in *The Wiz ... ard of Oz*. The expressions locked on their faces are shock and awe. Then they both begin blinking rapidly, and suddenly their chins fall to their chests. It's as if their operating systems have crashed and shut down. It doesn't take long for them to reboot though. Their heads begin to slowly raise. Mindy looks at Elizabeth, they smile, look at me, and start crying. Shit! White woman tears! I also somehow know in my six minutes old, Black woman bones, that nothing is more powerful or more dangerous.

They begin again slowly walking forward. I uproot my feet and keep pace, step for step, walking backward. I can feel my back growing ever closer to the far wall.

Through steaming tears, crooked smiles, and perfectly capped straight teeth they say, "Sis, why can't we touch your hair?"

"Chile, my Black friend lets me touch her hair."

"Giiiirlfriend, stop tripping. All hair matters."

My left heel touches the back wall and like an Olympic swimmer I use it to spring forward. I push past them, their hands reaching and missing, and run out of the bathroom. As the door closes, through deep sobs, I hear them say, "I love your purse."

It's not a purse. Is it?

I run to my desk and collapse in my chair. I turn on my work computer and go to the source of all medical, paramedic, and diagnostic knowledge, We6MD. If anything knows what's happening to me, it will. Turns out I have Lupus, and/or Poison Ivy, and/or Cancer, and/or an aggressive case of hyperpigment-transgenderation. That last one feels made up. I'm just about to exit the page when my eye catches what looks like it could be words on the bottom of the site's landing page. I enlarge the screen and in print so small as to be almost unable to be seen, it reads, *Disclaimer: Pursuant to being Black AND Woman: For all diagnosis: If you feel pain, you don't. If it's life threatening, it's not. If you die from being ignored, unheard, or unbelieved, you didn't. We use cookies to collect data on your non-pain and un-death. Void nowhere.* I sigh, and before I can take another full breath I feel a hand on my shoulder. I turn with a start, sure that Mindy, Elizabeth, and their weaponized tears have found me. No. It's Ryan, my boss, and he's standing oddly close to me. Then I realize it's not his hand on my shoulder, it's his Khaki clad crotch.

6.

Cassandra Lawson. Four years ago I was hired to work at Accounting Specialized Systems. I've since had a meteoric rise up through the ranks and now hold the title of Accounts Specialist. My ascension has been in no small part thanks to one of the women set to be

133

promoted ahead of me getting pregnant. She got to have a baby and I got to have her place in line for promotion. The other reason I was promoted is Cassandra Lawson.

Cassandra actually trained me when I was a newly hired accounting clerk with Accounting Specialized Systems. She was a ball of light and knowledge. Where I'd graduated middle of the pack from a liberal arts state school, she'd graduated top of her class from Yale. On the CPA exam she'd scored 88 on the FAR, 90 on the AUD, 95 on the REG, and a perfect 99 on the assurance specialization section. I'd certainly passed the CPA but there is no need for us to go into my scores. No need at all.

Cassandra was easily the smartest, most intuitive, and wittiest person in the building. When people would say, numbers don't lie, she'd laugh and say, "You just need a better accountant." She seemed to just know a deeper truth about the language of accounting and numbers, and could manipulate both in a way that bordered on magic, on witchcraft. Besides being a funny, genius, ball of light, Cassandra was also a five foot one inch tall Black woman, who routinely wore three inch heels that somehow made her seem seven foot tall.

During my training she and I spoke about work a lot, and life a bit. I gleaned pieces of her story. From west Philadelphia she was born and raised. You can try to not sing the rest of the song but it's too late. You're already singing it in your head. Her family didn't have much money but put a strong emphasis on education. She was told that in a place filled intentionally with pitfalls, snares, and traps, education was her best way up, over, and out. She heard, she heeded, and she graduated high school with a 4.9 GPA. This caught the eye of a Yale affirmative action recruitment officer.

She was offered, and accepted, a full ride to Yale based on her scholastics. What should have been a rigorous, but joyous, matriculation through the Ivy League education system was spoiled by daily taunts from White legacy students. Almost daily, students whose qualifications for admission often consisted only of bloodlines and checkbooks insisted that she didn't belong. That she'd taken a slot that rightfully belonged to some else. A White someone else. That she was a charity case. That she was invalid, illegitimate, an interloper. She said that while growing up, and confronting bullies on the playground, her mother had always told her, "It's not what they call you, it's what you answer to." So she didn't answer when they called her welfare queen, Aunt Jemima, or the Black girl. No. But she answered fully and completely the afternoon she was called to the podium as Valedictorian of her graduating class.

Cassandra was hired two years before I was. She was second in line for the promotion I eventually got. That was before number one got pregnant and last year's office Christmas party.

The Accounting Specialized Systems annual Christmas party lives somewhere between a frat boy bacchanal and a steamy Caribbean fete. A steamy Caribbean fete? Who even am I? Anyway, there's music, cocaine, dancing, cocaine, hors d'oeuvres and cocaine fueled behavior. It was not to be missed. Literally. Attendance was mandatory.

Everyone was there. Almost everyone was high. I remember

dancing with Mindy, my hand halfway up her dress, and seeing Cassandra run out. I thought nothing of it. The next day though it was all anyone could whisper about. Cassandra had run out of the party and to the police claiming that Ryan had sexually assaulted her.

At the party, on her way to the women's restroom, Ryan had grabbed her and pulled her into the men's restroom. She struggled against him. She screamed for help. Other men, men she knew, entered the bathroom, relieved themselves, washed their hands, and left. Her fight and plight went unacknowledged as Ryan all but raped her.

While his hands groped and grabbed, his foot slipped on the urine splattered floor. He lost balance for a second, and in that moment she was able to put a three inch heel into his groin. He collapsed in a heap on the floor, still reaching out for her, as she escaped into the night.

A police report was filed. A complaint made. Lawyers were hired. Bad publicity began to swirl. A settlement that came with a gag order was offered. A settlement that came with a gag order was accepted. Cassandra, her wit, expertise, and light, was gone. She became the Voldemort of A.S.S., She-Who-Is-Not-To-Be-Named, and I became the Accounts Specialist.

The morning of the office Christmas party she cornered me in the break room and told me that Ryan had said, and done, things to her that were inappropriate. I had not only ignored her, I didn't believe her. Some of the things she'd said Ryan had done, I'd done to women before. So it couldn't be wrong. She was just taking it the wrong way. Too sensitive. Too uptight. Too angry. I told her to just relax. Boys will be boys. He was just kidding. Just having fun. Just what exactly had he done to her, I asked. She said it all started one day when he walked up behind her while she was working and put his crotch, his dick, on her shoulder.

I still remember the look of hurt, and anger in her eyes when she told me about the initial assault. As I look from my shoulder, to his crotch, to his eyes, I wonder if Ryan can see the hurt, and anger in mine.


7.

"You want it?" Ryan asks. His words come out in breathy, thick, huffs, like the first smokey exhausts of a diesel truck on a winter morning. His voice is as sweet and poisonous as antifreeze. His eyes are glazed over like the Hot and Ready light is on at Krispy Kreme. "What!?" I reply. My voice breaks with rage and confusion. He pushes himself more fully against me, making sure I feel his growing arousal. I stand quickly, as fast as I can, hoping that my shoulder will neuter him. He's fast, faster than he looks, faster than his size would suggest.

He jumps back, smooths the front of his khakis, and looks around to see who is watching. Who is witnessing. The eyes that do meet his immediately find something else to see. Their computer screens. The floor. The ceiling. Anything else. He clears his throat, raises his chin, and slowly walks forward. I pull Bing Cross-B in front of me as some sort of barrier between us. His index finger trails along the top of my cubicle as if checking it for dust. My hands ball into fists. He stops, begins shaking his head from side to side like a disappointed parent and says, "If you want to be considered for that promotion have those reports on my desk by the end of the day." Then he leans forward, out of arms reach and whispers, "If you want to be guaranteed that promotion have yourself at my apartment by the end of the night." He winks at me, turns, and walks away with a gleeful bop. In his retreat he finds the time to stop and wish others a good morning, like he didn't just ruin mine. Like he didn't just assault and threaten me.

I watch as he passes the elevator bank. My eyes narrow to slits. His words, *by the end of the night*, ring in my ears. My fists are balled so tightly my fingernails dig into my palms. My skin crawls remembering his unsolicited, unwanted, undesired touch. I pull my crossbody bag off and hold it in my right hand like the stone Cain used to slay Abel. I feel my weight shifting to the balls of my feet and the muscles in my calves turning into springs. I'm about to go after him. Just about to give him some unwanted touches of my own when I hear the elevator floor bell ding. The doors to the center elevator slide open, and life slows to a crawl. Oh my God. Stepping off the elevator, wearing a purse, is Gavin DeWitte. Me. I look at my computer. At the date. It's the day of the annual Christmas party, one year ago. The promotion. The woman in the bathroom mirror. I'm Cassandra Lawson.

8.

I stand frozen. I watch Gavin DeWitte exit the elevator, make small talk, and glad-hand his way, my way, through the office. Gavin throws his head back and laughs, his mouth wide, his molar cavities showing, at something Margaret says. He, I, clearly like Margaret because never in the history of laughter has she ever said anything THAT funny. My Lord, is that what my laugh sounds like? It's somewhere north of Will Smith's manic enthusiasm and south of Kawhi Leonard's maniacal insanity. A manic depressed Eddie Murphy with mesothelioma if you will.

I remember this day. I'm wearing the brown, pinstripe, pleated pants my ex bought me for my birthday two years prior. When I put them on and modeled them for her she immediately said that she should return them for a different cut. She said they made me look like I had child bearing hips. I told her she was being ridiculous. Turns out, she was right. Gavin looks like he's wearing jodhpurs, and he isn't.

Beneath a tan sweater Gavin, I, got from the back rack at The Dap he's wearing a sky blue shirt he, I, got from the back rack at Banana Democratic. The sweater is too big. Way too big. I'm clearly a medium sized man wearing an extra large sweater. I look like a boy that's been playing in his father's closet. Of course, for me, no outfit would be complete without Bing Cross-B. Which I must admit maybe, possibly, might be a purse. You couldn't have convinced me that I didn't look amazing. That I wasn't ready for the pages of *GQ*. Ready for New York fashion week. Ready to sashay down a back rack catwalk. Wow. You don't really know how you look until you see yourself through the eyes of a Black woman.

I, Gavin, walked off the elevator that day and saw Cassandra Lawson standing there staring at me. Her jaw slack. Her eyebrows raised to her hairline. I thought she was checking me out. Turns out she was checking me off. Ill-fitting pants? Check. Ill-fitting sweater? Check.

I remember. I nodded my head to her and held my chin a little higher knowing that I was the object of her admiration. I disappeared behind a grey partition and into the break room to make a cup of coffee. I'm having that thought just as Gavin nods to me, a sly grin on his face, and disappears into the break room. Is this what déjà vu is? Me, us, remembering a moment, a day, a life we've already lived as ourself, or someone else.

I jump up and chase after Gavin. I find him, me, standing by the coffee machine. I throw Bing Cross-B on the counter just behind him, take him by the shoulders, and spin him around. I'm face to face with myself. I can tell that I am confused by what I'm, what Cassandra, is doing. I'm cool with Cassandra but we've never interacted like this. I hear the desperation in my voice as I tell Gavin about Ryan. About what just happened. How it's not the first time. How I know it won't be the last. I search his steel grey eyes and I can see that … I don't believe me. I can tell that I'm not even really listening to myself. Gavin is just trying to be free of this moment, and far away from this conversation. My heart sinks.

When you were young did you ever tell yourself stories about what'd you do if someone was drowning in a lake? How, without regard for your own safety, you'd jump in and save them. How you'd walk out onto a ledge yourself just to talk a suicidal man off of one. That's the you, you imagine yourself to be. That's the you, you told yourself you were. A hero. That's the you, you've been promising the world that you

140

are. Strong. Resilient. Unwavering. As I stand there watching Gavin, watching myself, I know I'm not who I think I am. I know that I'm not who I hoped I'd be. My shoulders fall and I take a deep breath knowing that I'm not going to save me.

9.

Have you ever heard of the Grandfather Paradox? It explores that idea of you going back in time and killing your grandfather. It states that if you did, you'd by extension keep one of your parents from being born and thus you'd never exist. But you'd have to exist to commit the act, so the fact that you killed your grandfather proves that you do in fact exist. Thus the paradox. It's often used as a way of saying that time is immutable. That what will happen, will happen. That it has happened. You can throw a rock in a river and cause a ripple, but the river will correct itself, straighten out the ripple, and keep flowing in the same direction. Keep flowing to the same end. The Grandfather Paradox is more complicated than *Back to the Future* but not as complicated as *Tenet. Looper* if you will.

I live a day as Cassandra Lawson knowing what will happen by the end of the night. I walk from the break room back to my cubicle. I'm Anita Hill watching Clarence Thomas walk toward a can of Coke. I drive home at the end of the day. I'm Lauren Sivan being escorted by Harvey Weinstein to the kitchen of Cafe Socialista. I change into my dress for the party. I'm Beverly Johnson being offered a cappuccino by Bill Cosby. I walk into the Four Seasons ballroom. I'm Joan of Arc walking to the stake.

I push through the large double doors into a ballroom filled with strobing lights, people dancing poorly, and loud music that feels like an excuse for White people to rap-sing the word nigga. Hors d'oeuvres, champagne, and cocaine flow freely. I abstain from all. As I cross the dance floor faceless voices shout compliments over the music, and disembodied hands continuously reach for my hair. I walk near the men's room. I'm pulled in. I'm assaulted while men I know watch, and pretend not to see or know me. I kick Ryan, and run. I sprint back across the dance floor, my dress torn, my dignity left on a urine splattered floor. I see Mindy dancing with Gavin. His hand, my hand, is up her skirt. I'd thought Mindy liked it. Loved it. Running past I see the look on her face. Fear. Distress. I'm not who I think I am.

I burst, running, through the doors of the Four Seasons at full gait. I'm one block away when I notice the cool night air pushing streaking wetness across my face. I realize for the first time I'm crying, and have been crying. I'm two blocks away, my arms pumping, when my lungs begin burning from the effort of running. I'm three blocks away from the party, from the moment, when the hungry hands and empty eyes revisit me. I'm four blocks away, and my calves are on fire, when I see it. I almost run over it. A sign sits in front of a cart that reads, *BLACC KOFFEE: A Pop-Up*. I guess that's why they call them pop-ups, they appear out of nowhere.

10.

I stop running. My body aches as my chest heaves up and down in a search for air. Standing before me regal and resplendent, her jaw clenching and releasing around a piece of gum, is Olo-Dumara. When I encountered her before I said, I don't see color. I don't know if that was ever true but I know it's not true now. She's the color of the coffee. Rich. Brown. Bold. As if reading my thoughts Olo-Dumara looks at me, winks, and points to the part of her sign that reads, *Guaranteed to Change Your Life.* She smiles, her teeth as white and her smile as wide as the bubble she starts to blow. "Wait," I shout. "Is this real?" The bubble grows until it's all I can see. Through tears I scream, "Was any of that real? Tell me!" As the bubble expands I can see her face through it. Just as the bubble touches the tip of my nose, she winks, and the bubble bursts.

11.

I blink and raise my hand to shield my eyes from the sun. The sun? I turn my hand from my palm to the back. I stare at my skin and take in a deep breath. I'm White. I reach down, grab my crotch and exhale. I'm a White man! I hear a distant voice shout, "And the sky is blue! Check your privilege!" I look across the street into the face of an irritated Gen Z-er. I hadn't realized I'd declared my White manhood aloud. I look around and I'm sitting in the middle of a sidewalk. And I'm four blocks from my office. I stand, and look down at myself. I'm wearing tan khakis, brown loafers, a powder blue shirt and a navy blue sweater. My watch reads nine a.m. on the head. My knees buckle, my head starts to swim, and for a moment I think that maybe I better sit back down.

It's the exact day, and hour, and I'm standing on the exact same spot I was when I first encountered Olo-Dumara, and her Blacc Koffee. Did I? Wait? Did any of that happen? Did I just lose consciousness and imagine all of that? Why was I sitting on the ground? Oh shit! I must have passed out. And my bag is missing! Maybe I was robbed and knocked unconscious. After all, my bag is where I keep my wallet and keys. Yes. Yes! Being robbed makes more sense, and is more comforting, than thinking I've been time traveling as a Black woman. I look around, not entirely sure that Olo-Dumara isn't going to pop-up. I take a few deep breaths and slowly start walking toward the office.

I walk into the building as Brian, one of my co-workers, is walking out. I wave but he doesn't see me. Or maybe he does; he's a strange one. I scan my access badge and Bridgette, one of the many rotating armed guards in the lobby, says nothing. A muzak version of Michael Jackson's, "Man in the Mirror" begins playing as I step on the elevator. The elevator is mirrored. The walls, the ceiling, every surface except the floor (for HR reasons) is reflective. I catch a glimpse of myself and have to put my hand to my face to ensure it's me. It is. In color, gender, shape, and form. Or is it?

I exit the elevator just as Mindy and Elizabeth are walking past, toward the restroom. Mindy sees me and recoils. Her head ducks down, her shoulders raise, and her eyes go to the floor. The look on her face is one of fear and distress. I want to say something. Anything. But I don't know what to say. Just then I feel a hand on my shoulder, and hear Ryan's voice say, "You still want it?"

I turn quickly, knocking his hand off my shoulder. "What!?" I all but shout. Ryan looks at me completely befuddled. He takes a beat and says, "The ticket to the football game. Last week I told you I might have an extra and you said that if I do you wanted it. Well I do. You still want it?" I rub my hands over my eyes, and shake my head like a child waking from a long nap. "You okay?" Ryan asks. "Yes," I say and walk past him toward the break room. He shouts to my back, "Let me know *by the end of the day*."

I stumble into the break room. My breaths feel short. My chest feels tight. I lean against the counter and that's when I see it at the back, far end, of the counter. Bing Cross-B. I thought it'd been stolen. I open the bag and inside are two bags of coffee. Two bags of Blacc Koffee. I pick up one of the bags. On the label is Olo-Dumara blowing a bubble and winking. The packaging reads, *Koffee Will Make You Black Blend: Blacc Koffee is an immersive experience: Guaranteed to Change Your Life.* I immediately go over to the office coffee machine, a Kuisinpot Grind and Brew. I pour the beans into the grinder, and press the grind and brew button. Lights come on, begin to flash, and the machine whirls to life. Soon the hypnotic, bold, sweet, and floral scent of Blacc Koffee fills the break room and diffuses throughout the office.

Ryan comes into the break room, his head high. He follows the smell of the coffee like it's a trail of breadcrumbs leading him to a gingerbread house deep in a forest. He says, "That smells amazing! You just brew that?" I nod. "You mind if I grab a cup," he asks. I wink. He pours himself a mug, holds it up to his face, and lets the warmth wash over him. He looks up at me. His forehead creases, he eyebrows furrow, and he says, "Are you chewing gum?" My cheeks fill like John Coltrane center stage at The Five Spot, and I begin to blow a bubble.

# *Yellovely*

[Fiction]

# *Yellovely*
## [Fiction]

My boss, Aashi, is asking if I'm okay. I'm not. I'm standing on the other side of her desk, rattled, and squinting into the blinding sunlight pouring in through her floor to ceiling office windows. What, other than a jade plant, needs this much sunlight? Is Aashi secretly a jade plant? I've never seen a jade plant wear Tom Ford and Christian Louboutin so probably not.

I raise my left hand to shield my eyes from the glare and my shirt, wet with sweat, touches my back. The damp cold cotton brushing my warm skin makes me flinch a bit, like a small child being threatened with a tickle. I lower my arm and try to look, calm? Brave? Something other than how I feel. I don't think I've said anything yet. Aashi uses a remote to adjust the blinds so that I'm no longer blinded and asks again,

"Are you okay? What happened?"

I'm asking myself the same thing. I look past her into the muted light, and I begin to silently remember. Well, more like relive what happened.

It started at a traffic light. The purgatory light at the corner of Memorial and Covington. The tortoise could beat the hare, or former president trump could grow some hair, in the time it takes for that light to change. I was waiting on the green when the 3000 verse on "International Player's Anthem," started playing on the radio.

*"I sent a text to a girl I used to see..."*

Then the beat dropped, Pimp C came in, and how can you not dance in your seat to that? Jesus would have turned water to Hennessy and c-walked on it if that song was playing. I was rapping loud, mean-mugging hard, bouncing to the beat, and living out some *Italian Job*, gangster rap, heist fantasy shit in my head. That's when I notice a metallic yellow car with tinted windows that were midnight- on-Mars-black, slowly pulling up beside me.

I can't even begin to tell you what the make or model of the car was. It could have been a Honda, Kia, Chevy, Ford, gas, electric or hybrid, it didn't matter. What made the car of note, eye-catching, and dare I say unforgettable was its unique shade of yellow. I'd never seen that color anywhere, on anything, ever. It was like the colors yellovely and quicksilver from the crayon box had a child out of wedlock, and that child grew up to be a make and model free car.

I also couldn't help but notice the no-way-that's-legal dark dark tint on the windows. In Georgia — be it man, beast, or motor vehicle — anything that dark is ostensibly against the law, and this was the Yaphet Kotto of tinted windows. The yellovely car pulled up along my driver's side, parallel, and then the passenger side window started to slowly roll down. For reasons I can't fully explain, it felt menacing. My back, and the hairs on my arm, sat up straight. Somewhere in the corner of my mind I heard Tre from *Boyz N The Hood* shouting, "Ricky!!"

The window inched and inched until finally it was completely down. The interior of the car appeared to be blacker than the tint. It was as if within this vehicle lived a black hole that just rode around pulling light, sound, joy, and Ricky into its nothingness. I squinted my eyes and craned my neck trying to get a better look. I moved my face closer to my, still rolled up, window trying to see inside the car. The first thing that escaped the all-consuming darkness of the vehicle was a sound, a sort of laughter. It was reminiscent of the cackle-like chuckle of the Joker in the old Batman cartoons. It was what I imagine the last noise an antelope hears just before a spotted hyena comes running out of the brush sounds like. The sound of danger, menace, and death.

As if conceived in a bottomless pit and birthed from pitch itself, the top of a head crowned out of the darkness, and pushed its way into the light. The head turned suddenly and a face appeared. The driver was leaning all the way across into the passenger seat and must have also been wearing nothing but black because the head that appeared seemed disembodied. Like the headless horseman's head had somehow financed a car. Then this seemingly body-less head smiled at me. It wasn't the warm and inviting smile of a beautiful stranger. It was the terrifying and unnerving smile of a feral and deranged possum. I grabbed the wheel with both hands, looked straight ahead, and felt the first drops of sweat forming beneath my shirt. Before I recoiled I noticed that the smile belonged to a woman. Maybe she was Latina, possibly a Black woman, could have been a White woman. I didn't look very long. Most people's smile makes you want to smile too. Hers did not.

Out of the corner of my eye I could see a hand waving, trying to get my attention. The disembodied head came with a hand. Like the Headless Horseman's head and Cousin It somehow financed a car. I

150

ignored the hand waving. I couldn't believe the damn light hadn't changed! The hand began waving with more energy, like an old school hip hop artist had demanded that she raise her hand in the air and wave it like she just didn't care. I took a deep breath, and smiled the smile you smile when your mom makes you stand beside Aunt Brenda (who kind of smells like sharp cheddar wrapped in feet), pulls out a camera and says, "Say cheese!" And you inadvertently say, "Feet!" I smiled *that* smile and turned toward the hyper hand. The waving immediately stopped.

I glanced to see if the light had changed. It hadn't. The woman's hand slowly and methodically formed itself into a fist, and then just as slowly she extended her index finger. My eyes were moving between the hand and the traffic light like they were caught in an extended rally at the US Open. I was strongly considering running the light but the early morning traffic was as thick as Magic City dancers eating JR Crickets wings. There was no break in the steady stream of cross traffic. I looked back just as the extended index finger moved to the right corner of the driver's mouth, then drew an imaginary U through the chin, and to the left corner of the driver's mouth. Once the U was complete the driver smiled even wider, pointed to me, and through clenched teeth laughed her cartoon Joker laugh. The light turned and like a deadbeat dad, I took off.

I raced down Memorial Drive and jumped on 285. I was well into the flow of traffic before I was able to breathe my first sigh of relief. I took in a full breath, the recycled-pine-tree-freshened air and toxic fumes from my engine never tasted so sweet. I mean, they tasted like mesothelioma, but the sweet kind. I let deep breath air rest in the dregs of my lungs. After a moment I exhaled in a way that I hadn't since, allegedly, smoking what I thought to be that good good, but what was really that low mid, in college. It was that breath, and the ease I felt on the other side of it, that let me know how truly uneasy and up on my hind legs I'd been during the exchange. What the fuck was that about! And why was it so, weird! Strange! Scary! What was I scared of? A racially ambiguous woman in a yellovely car with a Mark Hamill laugh? I started laughing, imitating hers until the ridiculousness of it made me break into genuine laughter, and that then sent me into a coughing fit. Probably a remnant and result from, allegedly, smoking all that low mid in college, or mesothelioma. I was starting to think about how I was pissed that I missed the rest of "International Player's Anthem" especially the end of the Big Boi verse,

*"Better choose the right one or pick, pick the kiddies up."*

That's when I spotted a flash of a uniquely metallic yellow, roughly ten car lengths behind me, weaving through traffic, and gaining fast.

I told myself that it couldn't be the same car. What other car could it have been though? I'd never seen anything with that particular hue of yellow before. A hue of yellow that appeared to be hopping through the morning traffic like it was a real life game of Frogger. Unconsciously my foot began to rest more heavily on the gas pedal. I may not have known the make or model of the car the cartoon-Joker-laughing, oddly menacing, racially ambiguous, disembodied-headed woman was driving but I did know that I was driving a red 2005 Dodge (not Plymouth) Neon. Not only do they no longer make parts for the 2005 Dodge Neon, they don't even make the car! My Neon is more wildebeest with a broken leg, gout and asthma, than fleet footed antelope. This was evidenced by the fact that the yellovely car was at that moment right on my bumper.

When I sped up the yellovely car sped up. When I slowed down it slowed down as well. The car was so close to my bumper it was damn near in my trunk; it was damn near a spare tire, and a McDonalds bag I should have thrown out months ago. There was nothing I could do so I just drove and tried to ignore the car. This was easier said than done.

Have you ever gotten off on the Candler Road exit and had the water boys, the kids selling water at the stop lights, run up to your car? They're shouting,

"Fuck with me Unc!"

"Get some water pops with your thirsty ass!"

"You and this ashy ass car look dehydrated folk! Get some water in both of ya!"

Sales pitches that are equal parts true and rude. Those kids sometimes, most times, get so close that you can see, feel, and damn near smell their breath through the window. There is a desperation and need in their voices that makes you want to lock your already locked door. Just push the lock button again just for good measure. You don't but you want to. You know what I mean? It would be easier to ignore those kids than it was to ignore that car. It was so close to my bumper that I looked like I was towing it. Just then the metallic yellow car hit its brakes, pulled hard to my left, laid on the gas and pulled up beside me, again, parallel.

Two months ago a woman gave a man the finger on I-75/85 after he honked at her for apparently driving, what he felt to be, too slowly in the fast lane. Data from her GPS later confirmed that she was actually driving ten over the posted speed limit. Outraged by her one finger salute he tailed her. She exited at 10th and got caught at the light. He pulled up parallel to her car, exited his, ran over, broke her window with his bare fist, and punched her in the face. This was all caught on a traffic cam.

Three weeks ago a man in a red F-150 cut off another man in a white Malibu on 75 south. What had been a minor inconvenience then turned into an angry game of, who can speed up and cut whom off the fastest. It was a rainy day in Atlanta. The gentleman in the white Malibu sped up in an effort to perform a third extremely dangerous, and petty, re-cut off. This time the Malibu clipped the front bumper of the red pick-up truck. The impact caused the Malibu to fishtail. The driver lost control. The car skidded off the road and began to flip and roll as it disappeared into the flowering dogwood trees near the Forest Park exit. The man in the Malibu had his entire family in the car with him. He was the only one to survive the wreck. The driver in the red F-150 never stopped. This was all captured by a combination of traffic cams, and footage from cellphones recorded by people who stopped to record but didn't stop to help.

Two days ago a man in a Sentra, while distracted on his cell phone, bumped into the back of a matte black Charger. It was a minor fender bender. The driver of the Charger exited and shot the driver of the Sentra to death. This murder was caught on cell phone, posted to social media, and viewed a million times before it was taken down.

Today I had a yellovely car paralleling me on 285.

This laundry list of violent and deadly road rage incidents cataloged themselves as I stared straight ahead and tried to ignore the car keeping pace with me on my left. I didn't know if the driver was insane, armed, or what she wanted. Then a single tear welled up, fell from my left eye, and ran down my cheek. It wasn't a tear of fear, or sorrow, but one of anger and frustration.

Have you ever had an older, stronger sibling hold you against the ground, and no matter how much you struggled and fought you couldn't push them off? You couldn't get away. Have you ever had that kind of frustration and anger drive you to tears? Maybe it wasn't a sibling. Maybe it was a test that you studied hard for but when you sat to take it you realized immediately that you didn't know any of the answers. Maybe it was a marriage that no matter how hard you tried to make work, just kept getting worse. Maybe it was year three of walking into a dead end job... or MAYBE it was an asshole sibling after all. Whatever the cause it was that feeling of being trapped, pinned, and powerless with no way out that drove you to frustrated and angry tears. That's how I was feeling, boxed in and pissed.

More tears rose from the well behind my eyes and my vision started to blur. Before I could stop myself I rolled my window down and shouted at the car,

"What! What the fuck do you want! WHAT!!"

The yellovely car immediately lurched as if to ram the side of my car! I pulled hard right pushing my passenger side tires to the edge of the shoulder. The yellovely car then, just as suddenly, went back into its own lane and began slowing down. One car length away, two car lengths back, until it disappeared like that white Malibu into the flowering dogwoods.

I pulled back into my lane. My hands were shaking so badly you'd have thought I had spirit fingers. I was confused by what had just happened. I was driving fast, maybe too fast, like I was still being chased. My eyes kept going to the rear view mirror, like a tongue to where a tooth used to be. I was this way, paranoid and tense, until I pulled into the office parking lot. I pulled into my parking space, turned the car off, and reminded myself to breathe. There was a stillness, peace, and quiet in the car, that I guess always existed when the car was motionless, that I'd never noticed before. It felt like church, like sanctuary, like safety. I took off my hat. I forgot I was even wearing one. The hat band was wet with sweat. I looked at my reflection in the mirror behind the visor and you'd have thought I'd just run a marathon. I felt like I looked older, and more haggard just from the stress of the morning. I looked down and the pits of my shirt were stained through. I lifted my arm and gave a sniff. I was a little musty, not fully funky, just a little musty. I was going to have to change shirts before I went to my desk; maybe head down to the office gym and shower. I lifted the visor back up and rolling toward me slowly like a hyena whose prey thought it had escaped only to discover it was now cornered, was the yellovely car.

The car crept up beside mine and stopped once our driver's side windows were directly across from one another. Parallel. She just let the car idle. The only sound in the parking lot was the purr of her car's engine. I wanted to drive off but I was frozen. I was frozen more out of pride than fear. I was not going to be run off by some woman. No! I didn't know what, in the absence of driving off, to do. So I did nothing. I gripped the steering wheel, and clenched my jaw. Out of the corner of my eye I watched as the window to the car came down. I heard the laughter first. How could something meant to signify joy sound so evil? Her laughter sounded like, what I imagine, the fallen angels heard after Satan was told his first joke in hell. The disembodied head slowly emerged. I let go of the wheel, rolled down my window, turned, and faced her.

I hadn't really seen her face in traffic but sitting there, the sound of an idling engine serving as the soundtrack, I took note of her. She was young. Twenty five maybe. Certainly not yet thirty. She was bald. I still couldn't place her race. Her complexion wasn't so much tanned, or brown, as it was jaundiced yellow. Her lips were a thin line. Her face, a blank slate, smooth almost devoid of features. Her eyes were almost perfectly round with the fire Prometheus stole from the God's burning in them. Her nose was keen and her nostrils pinpoints you could almost miss. She appeared to possibly have on black eyeliner, but no other makeup. The fact that little about her face was of note, was notable. She could be anyone, any woman.

She raised her right hand, quickly, to the right corner of her mouth. The suddenness of her movement made me jump in spite of myself. She once again extended her index finger and drew an imaginary U from the right corner of her mouth, through her chin, to the left corner. Then she smiled wide, pointed to me, and through clenched teeth laughed. The wide smile and laughter made the burning fire in her eyes blaze even brighter.

"Why aren't you smiling?"

The words leaked from behind her smile like a deadly gas. Her teeth were still clenched tight. Her voice was deeper than I would have imagined, but it was a perfect complement to her laugh.

"Excuse me?" I replied, indignantly.

Without meaning to, I'd added a little extra bass to my voice. Maybe I meant to.

"Why. Aren't. You. SMILING?" she said again as if sounding out a word.

Smiling was, clearly, said with more force than the other words.

"Smiling for what?" I replied, the extra bass fading a bit.

"Smiling because I'm asking you to. Smiling because you're more handsome when you smile. Smile for me!"

Talking through clenched teeth had caused drool to pool at the corners of her mouth, and run down her chin. She didn't appear to care. She just kept her fiery eyes on me.

"You stalked me for fifteen miles for a smile! A fucking smile! Fuck you!"

Somewhere in the darkness of her car I saw what I can only assume was her left hand move. In that hand I saw a glint of metal. I couldn't see it clearly. I couldn't be sure of what it was.

"Is that a gun!?" I asked as the last of the faux bass left my voice and I explored the higher heights of falsetto.

She leaned forward.

"Could be. Could be not. Either way though, wouldn't it be better to smile?"

The drool was running down her chin and falling onto her turtleneck.

Have you ever told yourself about the acts of bravery you'd commit when, and if, faced with certain dangers or impending perils. How you'd run into a burning building to save a baby. Never mind the fact that you can't even eat pizza that's too hot. Reality rarely creeps into the detail of one's hero fantasies. However, sitting there facing what "could be" or "could be not" a gun I felt the requested smile forcing its way into the corners of my mouth. A sad, nervous, and scared smile.

"What's going on here!?"

The voice of a fast approaching, golf cart driving, security guard caught us both by surprise. The yellovely car driver widened her smile, and wiped her chin while rolling up her window. She sped away, leaving only the smoke from her spinning tires and a set of skid marks on the pavement as evidence that she'd ever been there. I leaned back hard against my seat, panting, my chest heaving, my heart racing. I felt more sweat soaking into my already sweaty shirt. I could not have cared less. I just sat there and closed my eyes for a second, gathering myself.

I opened my eyes just as the security officer's golf cart pulled beside my car. Parallel. I looked over and read her name tag, Basma.

"Are you okay Mister..." she waited for me to catch my breath.

"Indoda. My last name is Indoda.

"Are you okay Mister Indoda?"

"I am now thank you officer Basma."

"Who was that? In the car."

"I don't know. Did you get the plate?"

"I did. G4GANDR. Is that familiar to you?"

"No. I've never seen that car or the driver before. I'm indebted to you for coming out when you did."

"It was your boss."

Basma pointed up to the top floor, corner office.

"She called down to the security desk and asked me to have you come up to her office."

"Wow! That was an incredibly heads up play by Aashi!"

"Indeed. I'll escort you to her office now if you're ready."

"No need. I know the way."

"I'll at least escort you to the building. We don't know if that car is just circling and waiting to come back when you're alone."

I heard that Joker's laugh, and saw that drooling smile in my mind, and shuddered.

"Okay. Okay," I said.

Officer Basma saw me safely into the building and I immediately went upstairs.

So, here I am, standing in Aashi's office still a bit shaken. I haven't answered her question and I'm sure the silence is starting to feel, odd. I look at Aashi for the first time. Initially I was blinded by the light, and then I got lost in my own thoughts. Aashi sits with her fingers tented beneath her chin. I turn, walk over to her floor to ceiling office window and look down to where my car is parked.

"Aashi, how did you see what was happening from all the way up here?" I ask.

"What was happening?" she responds with genuine confusion in her voice.

I turn and walk back to her, my eyebrows raised, my damp shirt sticking to my back,

"There was a woman in a yellow-ish car threatening me in the parking lot."

"Oh my God! You were threatened. No, I didn't see any of that," she says, her voice going from genuine confusion to deep concern.

"You didn't see that?"

"No."

Now it's my turn to be confused,

"Then why did you have security come out and check on me? Why did you ask me to come to your office? Why are you asking if I'm okay?"

Aashi stands, rounds her mahogany desk, and sits on its corner. She folds her arms across her chest, takes a deep breath and says,

"Because, from all the way up here, I noticed you weren't smiling."

Aashi raises her right hand, quickly, to the right corner of her mouth. She extends her index finger and draws an imaginary U from the right corner of her mouth, through her chin, to the left corner. Then she points to me, and through clenched teeth and a smile with a little bit of drool in its corners she asks,

"Why aren't you smiling Mr. Indoda?"

# *The Curio Case of Benson Stone*

[Fiction]

# The Curio Case of Benson Stone
## [Fiction]

1.

"I hope they have a level two charger hookup for the car and not that level one bullshit. Those level ones man, Jesus. You're talking fifteen hours to fully charge sometimes," Douglas says this aloud, in his full voice.

Douglas has a voice that is authoritative, and self-assured. It's the voice he searched for while being bullied in elementary school and found while playing sports in high school. It's the voice he now uses when arguing cases before judges and juries, trying to get his clients acquitted and cleared of all charges. It's a voice that has only ever been defeated in court once. Douglas tightly grips the steering wheel of his red, one hundred thousand dollar, Electric Thunderstroke. Until a moment ago the drive had been in complete silence. No favorite songs, no Moth Radio Hour, no conversation. Just the sound of Sumitomo tires gripping and releasing mile after mile of open highway. Douglas stares down the road, literally and figuratively, looking at everything.

Desdemona, sits staring out of the passenger-side window seeing everything but not really looking at anything. Every now and again she'll glance at her phone, and scroll through snapshots of other people's lives. Lives that look and feel far different from her own.

It never ceases to amaze her that Douglas finds the energy to complain about a car that he insisted they get. She knows that the only reason he purchased this one hundred thousand dollar Duracell on wheels is because Wallace, Douglas's college roommate, got a ninety thousand dollar lake blue, Electric Levin, and Douglas doesn't like to be upstaged.

Desdemona sits with her heels on the edge of the seat's cushion, her knees in her chest, and her arms wrapped around her knees. Sitting this way has always made her feel comforted and safe. Small and hidden. During thunderstorms as a child, as a teenager when her parents would fight, and in high school and college during bad break-ups she could be found in a chair, on a couch, or in her bed, a bundle of self-preservation, rocking with her knees hugged tightly to her chest.

She knows that Douglas has said what he's said, how he's said it, not just to complain about the car, but to break the deafening silence of the trip. It's an effort to spark conversation between them. An attempt to rekindle and catch fire logs that have laid cold in the hearth too long. She's been trying to do better. Trying to find the words that hide beneath her tongue and between her teeth. It's been hard. They have been slow to give up their hiding places. But she's been trying to coax them out.

Desdemona and Douglas met while arguing opposite sides of a state corruption case. Two lawyers finding word after word to best each other before a jury that could go either way. All in an effort to see justice, or some version of it, served. At least that's what they told themselves. In closing arguments they both spoke with passion and conviction but ultimately her words proved more potent and effective.

She prevailed. His only loss. It was also, oddly, the beginning of their courtship.

Their first date was a series of unfortunate events that would have made Daniel Handler jealous. Reservations were missed, tickets were lost, at one point police were called, and these two lawyers made a run for it. The date ended in a parking lot with Douglas's car booted, and a huge red wine stain in Desdemona's dress. It was in that moment that Douglas took Desdemona's hand in his, looking deeply into her eyes, and paid her what was at the time his highest compliment,

"You're an amazing litigator. Maybe the best I've ever seen."

Desdemona not sure if he was being serious, never the best at taking a compliment, still winded from running from the cops, and slightly offended by the "maybe" punched him in the arm and replied,

"I know you are but what am I?"

They laughed, he massaged his arm, they kissed, and a year later they were engaged. A year after that married. In those two years they'd spoken often of their desire to have children and build a family. So when she discovered she was pregnant it seemed like a dream. And when she miscarried six months later it felt like a nightmare. A nightmare that left them floating in a sea of silence, slowly drifting apart, and searching for the right words to shore up their relationship.

They'd had a few breakthrough moments in therapy but those moments didn't seem to live on the other side of their therapist's door. Then, Tina, their therapist suggested they get away. Suggested that disconnecting from the world might be just what they need to reconnect

166

to each other. Douglas told Wallace. Wallace suggested he and his wife Doran, and Douglas and Desdemona, all rent cabins and spend the weekend fishing and swimming on Lake Siri. Douglas said yes immediately. Desdemona felt less sure, but here they were zero emission-ing their way to a cabin getaway.

"You okay," Douglas asks, his voice soft and concerned.

It's the voice he uses late at night, when it's just the two of them with the sandman's dust in their eyes, and their pillows singing them lullabies.

"Yes, why do you ask?"

Desdemona turns and sees that he's staring at her hands, which are tented tightly across her midsection, her phone sandwiched in-between. She hadn't realized that she'd let go of her legs and had begun cradling her stomach. Desdemona takes her feet off the seat, sits on her hands and phone, takes a deep breath, and red rovers some words.

"Fifteen hours to recharge huh. What would you do with those fifteen hours other than charge the car, Dougie?"

Desdemona looks over, winks at Douglas, and smiles knowing that she is the only person he will tolerate calling him Dougie. He looks over just in time to catch her wink. That smile and that wink were the catalyst for his only courtroom loss. Without a doubt he married the most charming and charismatic woman he's ever known.

"Desi," Douglas says, his eyes going back to the road.

Desi has been what he's called her since their first date.

"Fifteen hours? It takes fifteen hours to make a delicious brisket not charge a car. No. No. No!"

Douglas smiles, and again glances over at his wife. Her sun bleached blonde hair sways with the rhythm of the road, and lightly brushes her tanned shoulders like an index finger trying to get someone's attention. Shadows kaleidoscope across her face as the sun streams through the leaves of the dense Spanish Moss laden tree branches that hang over head. He's struck by how beautiful she is. He's ashamed that lately he hasn't really been looking at her. Since the miscarriage everything has been head buried in work and nose to the grindstone. Thoughts of the next house and the next car. Things that he's given the impossible task of replacing the irreplaceable. Things to distract him from how hurt and, if he's honest, angry he's been feeling. So he told himself that he was blindly pursuing these things because they both wanted them. But maybe, actually, it was just him trying not to face the truth. Douglas's right hand leaves the wheel and settles high on her left thigh. He swallows hard.

"...Uhm... I ... I can think of other things we could do with fifteen hours too."

Desdemona feels her body tense and go rigid. Douglas does too, and quickly takes his hand away. They've tried but haven't found the comfort, ease, and desire to be intimate. Not since. She knows that 'they' is mostly 'her.' He's made overtures, and she's made excuses.

She looks over at Douglas. His broad shoulders that once captained a high school football team to the city championship. His

168

forearms that though relegated to pushing pencils still hint at a strength that's not to be tested. His square jaw and cleft chin. His high cheekbones, and sun tanned skin. His round brown eyes that push into slits when he laughs. The handsome face of a man that was once her adversary. The handsome face of her husband.

She can still feel how warm his hand was on her thigh, and now her thigh feels warmer as well. She's been hurt and angry too. She left her job with the firm when she found out she was pregnant, to prepare for the baby. In the aftermath there was no job, and no baby, just him. So he became the recipient of all her hurt, of all her confusion, of all her ire. She wasn't mad at him. She was mad at the world, but the world never sat at the dinner table so that she could give it a piece of her mind. He did.

Desdemona exhales and feels her jaw and body relax. She'd been grinding her teeth again. She takes Douglas's hand and places it higher on her thigh, and puts her hand gently atop his,

"The property rental agent assured me, level two. But if we're lucky, maybe she's wrong."

She gives his hand a gentle squeeze. His hand, once warm, is now red hot.

Douglas looks over and says,

"Well... maybe they have a level one mattress as well."

They simultaneously erupt into laughter, something they haven't done for far too long.

2.

There are roads of such length and width that they seem to lead everywhere. There are also roads so long and wide you don't feel like they're going anywhere. The road Desdemona and Douglas are on feels like the latter. Each mile seems to bleed into the next until one might ask one's self, didn't we just pass that? Douglas knows they are somewhere near the mountains. He's seen pictures but he's never been in this area, or on these roads himself. He can't deny that the scenery, in all directions, is green, lush, vibrant, and beautiful. It's Garden of Eden picturesque. He thinks to himself, however, that he'd have eaten the apple and gotten kicked out of the garden too if this was all there was to it.

"Oh shit!" Desdemona exclaims lifting her cellphone high against the car's ceiling.

"What? What happened? Is everything okay!?"

Douglas instinctively begins to slow down just in case they need to turn around. Their home burglar alarm may have alerted her phone of a robbery, or maybe she got a text saying something happened to one of her parents, or...

"No, it's... I was looking at a post on InstaFace and lost reception."

Douglas lets out a long breath, loosens his grip on the steering wheel, chuckles, and replies, "Oh No. No!" He begins shaking the steering wheel left to right making the car writhe in the road, "Not a loss of social media! How will we survive Desi! Desi what will we do!!" He laughs and continues, "How will we show that we like things, and each other, if we can't double click on something, anything!" He howls. Tears start to form in his eyes as his laughter grows into shoulder bouncing convulsions.

"Stop it Douglas!" Desdemona shouts, feinting anger while reluctantly sniggering. My God it feels good to laugh, and tease, and play like we used to, she thinks. Desdemona felt unsure about the weekend cabin stay, but is feeling more and more sure they've made the right decision. She continues searching the ceiling for a signal, "It's not funny, Dougie!"

She leans into him, her shoulder playfully jostling his. He shakes the steering wheel from side to side again as if the impact has Herculean. The car continues to playfully pitch, and now they're both caught in a full laugh.

Just then the digital voice in his phone intones, "*GPS Signal Lost.*" All laughter ceases. Douglas pulls the car over to the shoulder and starts searching for a signal on his phone as well. There is none.

"Uhm... how are we even going to get to the cabin?" Desdemona asks, already turning and looking back the way they came. Already feeling the tension returning to her body, and her teeth starting to grind.

"I can get us there," Douglas says with surprising surety as he rests his phone in his lap.

"Uhhh, how about we go back up the road until we get a signal and figure it out from there."

"I've got it, Desi. The directions are still in the phone. We turn on Seneca, which should be about three miles up. Then we turn on Oscarville and our cabin is somewhere down there."

Douglas eases the car off the shoulder and continues up the road. Desdemona places her left hand high on his right thigh.

"Okay. It's kinda sexy when you get all Marco Polo."

"I think of myself as more of a Magellan"

"I know you are but what am I?" They look at each other and smile. "Alright then Dougie, take me down to a paradise city where the grass is green and the lake is pretty."

3.

There are roads that, like life, change quickly and dramatically. Roads that transform so rapidly, so drastically, that by the time you notice one change you're well into another. After turning off the main road neither Douglas nor Desdemona could tell you exactly when the path they were on went from smooth pavement, to crunchy gravel, to uneven dirt. But it did. Neither Douglas nor Desdemona could tell you when the sun went from drowsy and rising from its slumber, to high and proud in the sky, to threatening to hide behind the horizon's dark skirt. But it had.

As the road grows long, and the sky goes from blue to purple to red, Douglas's face remains a mask of confidence and strength, but his left foot taps nervously as it keeps pace with his racing heart. He begins to feel unsure and uneasy. He could never admit that to Desdemona, or to anyone, ever. The road they'd turned down was where the last signal of the GPS had said it would be, three miles ahead, but there were no markers or road signs. Douglas is not entirely sure they were even on Seneca Road. He grips the wheel and is just about to turn around when he sees something up ahead.

It appears to be a person.

**4.**

"There's a man up ahead," Desdemona says, her voice cautious, her finger pointing as if picking someone out of a line-up.

She watches as the man up ahead smiles wide, whittles on a piece of wood, and gently and slowly sways back and forth in a rocking chair. He moves like the pendulum of a grandfather clock, mesmerizing, and hypnotic. Douglas slows the car to a crawl, like a nervous child inching toward a slightly cracked closet in the dark. As the vehicle grows closer Douglas begins to take note of the enormous tree just behind the rocking man.

It's a massive tree, unavoidably so, and yet Douglas hadn't noticed it until after he saw the man. The tree appears primeval. As if it isn't just *a* tree but *the* tree. Like there was none before this one, and will be none after. The trunk is as wide as all outside. So wide, so inescapable, it looks like a wallpaper plastered against the world. The bark is the brown of danced in mud puddles the day after a hard rain. The texture of the bark appears rough and cracked, like the palms of hands that lay brick for a living; knotted, with deep, and dark grooves that look to have no end. Grooves like creases cut into the horizon. Grooves like the places where time tucks away its secrets. The tree's branches, long and spindly, stretch out like summer school classes. They twist, and swing in the breeze as if tickling the sky's chin. The leaves live high on the branches and are a striking crimson, like those of a Red Sunset Maple. But this is no maple. The leaves seem to disappear as they chameleon into the ever reddening sunset.

Douglas isn't sure if Desdemona has even noticed the tree. Her eyes are solely fixed on the man in the chair. She can't seem to look away from him.

He's not a young man. Not by a long shot. She couldn't venture a true guess at his age though. He could be seventy. He could be one hundred and seventy. But his eyes carry in them a glint of youth, a flicker of mischief. His face wears the same color and deep lines as the tree's bark. His skin muddied. Grooved. Wizened. The rocking man has no eyebrows and is as bald as the new moon. His jaw is outlined by a beard as patchy as the inner city, makeshift, empty lot football fields where Douglas learned to play, and twice as dirty. His clothes, a pair of nondescript overalls and a loosely buttoned cotton shirt with a chew stick in the breast pocket, are both weathered and worn as if they've come from nature and are in the process of returning. He wears no shoes. His wide smile reveals teeth that are as white as Wyoming. As white as a hungry wolf's. He rocks to whatever rhythm is making the tree's branches swing.

As Douglas and Desdemona draw ever closer she can hear him singing. The song feels old in her ears, in her spirit. Like a vesper whispered softly in a past life. Like a graveside hymn sang loudly, long ago, as a shovel full of dirt fell on her placid face. Her foot begins to tap to the rhythm of the trees, to the rocking of the chair. The song moves with a pace that is urgent but not in a hurry, reminiscent of Robert Johnson's "Crossroad Blues." It feels dark and consuming. Like a dirge. It makes her want to run, and dance, and pray, at the same time. She doesn't know the song but it feels so familiar. Like she already knows the words.

The road splits into a Y where the man sits rocking, singing, and whittling, and the tree sits imposing, stretching, and swaying. Douglas and Desdemona don't know which arm of the Y will lead them to their cabin, or if they are even on the right road. They begin asking themselves, why. Why have their phone signals died? Why do these roads have no markers? Why is this man smiling at them?

The car sidles up beside the rocking man, and comes to stop. He is just outside of the driver's side window but now Douglas realizes that he isn't smiling at them at all. He's looking into the distance, at the horizon, at tomorrow and smiling. He doesn't turn to acknowledge their presence. He just rocks. Douglas rolls his window down. Still nothing. Maybe the man is blind, deaf. Douglas clears his throat and everything seems to stop. The man stops rocking. The tree branches stop swaying. The man stops smiling. The fading day suddenly feels still, as if time itself has been halted.

"Excusss," Douglas's always strong and confident voice cracks a bit.

He squares his shoulders, remembers who he is, and clears his throat again.

"Excuse me," Douglas says in his full voice.

"Gesundheit," the formerly rocking man says in a voice that seems to have no age or gender.

Douglas didn't see the man's mouth move, and wonders if he's imagined the response. Douglas continues,

"... I'm sorry, What?"

"You don't have to be sorry. Gesundheit."

This time Douglas sees the slightest movement in the man's lips. If he's a ventriloquist then who's the dummy Douglas thinks to himself before responding,

"But I didn't sneeze."

Douglas chuckles, and looks quizzically over at Desdemona who is still intently and silently staring.

"I never said you did," the man replies matter-of-factly as he begins to rock again, which also appears to give the trees permission to sway.

Douglas is a man used to being spoken to with a certain deference. A man used to commanding attention, respect, and admiration. The rocking man's response strikes him as curt.

"Well, okay then," Douglas says with no humor.

Desdemona, feeling Douglas's growing ire, pulls herself from her trance, and interjects.

"We were wondering if you could help us?"

Desdemona reaches back into her past and conjures the smile that not only won Douglas's heart but the sash and title of Ryegrass Queen in her hometown's county fair three years in a row. She'd always felt that it was lucky for the other girls that she aged out of the competition or she'd be queen until this day. The hours spent waving from floats made of hay bales, and the muscle memory built by wooden rulers rapped across her knuckles, cause her to unconsciously gather her fingers into a paddle just in case she needs to give a pageant wave as well.

"That depends," the man says, clearly having never been to a county fair.

"... On?" Desdemona replies, her fingers going from pageant to plebeian, as her sash winning smile begins to crack and twitch at the corners.

"On what kind of help you need." The rocking man finds his smile again as Desdemona loses hers. "If you need help changing a tire I'm not the help, miss."

"Oh no, we don't need..."

Before Desdemona can finish her thought the man interjects.

"Or if you need help being honest with yourself, I'm not your Better Help."

He turns to Douglas as he finishes the sentence. This is the only move he's made thus far other than rocking. His smile is now as wide as the base of the tree. A challenge that feels oddly personal to Douglas rests in the man's tone and action.

"What? What's that supposed to mean!?" Douglas says reaching for the car door handle. Desdemona reaches across him and takes his hand into hers.

"No worries brother. Exactly, what kind of help do YOU need?"

the man says, still looking at Douglas.

"You know what, fuck this! And fuck you!"

Douglas attempts to free his hand from Desdemona's but she holds firm. With her free hand she caresses his jaw and turns his face to hers. She slides in close and whispers in his ear.

"Dougie, we have no idea where we are. It's starting to get dark. We have no phone signal. We..."

The man begins to sing once again, and whatever her next words were to be freeze in her throat never to thaw. Her eyes move past Douglas and fall on the block of wood the man is whittling away on. A piece of distressed walnut. It's more than that though. More than just a block of wood. It's a block of wood being transformed into a doll of some sort. A small, one foot tall, lifelike figurine of a child. A Black child. The rocking man's singing becomes markedly louder as the doll's features come into sharp relief. Cheekbones as high as the leaves in the tree's branches. A nose as wide as the tree's trunk. Lips as full as the noon day sun, and hair that though whittled wood looks like matted wool. The distressed walnut gives the doll's face a look of sadness, loss, and anger. Though in the process of being newly created the figurine looks tired, and weary, like it's already run this race, and lost.

The doll's most striking and jarring feature, however, is its full, round, piercing, white eyes. The eyes don't look carved, or painted, but alive. Like at any moment the lids might blink, and tears might fall. The almost too white eyes seem to find Desdemona, and follow her. They ask, they question, they accuse. Desdemona stares at the doll, and the doll eyes seem to stare back. Involuntarily her hands tent tightly across her stomach. The words to inquire about the doll are just about to emerge from the depths when Douglas's anger subsides.

The facts of their situation become too clear to him, he takes a deep breath and says,

"Okay, okay, okay. Do you know..." but before he can get the question out the man, still rocking and smiling, interjects.

"So it's not fuck this, and fuck me, then?"

"You know what!" Douglas's temper, never far from the surface, comes raging back.

Desdemona again wades in as the voice of reason.

"Dougie! I'm sorry sir..."

"Don't apologize to this..."

Desdemona talks over Douglas drowning out the expletives that were surely riding a wave to a curse filled shore.

"I apologize sir! It's been a long day. My husband and I are hungry and exhausted. Do you know where Oscarville Road is?"

With that the man's smile once again fades. He stops rocking. He stops whittling. His shoulders fall. He lets out a heavy sigh and just as he does the wind begins to pick up.

"Absolutely I do."

Desdemona takes note of the shift in his countenance, and the weather.

"... could you tell us?"

"I could, but do you really want to know?"

"Yes! I'll be damned! We really want to know!" Douglas shouts through the window.

"You may indeed be," the man says in a voice so soft the wind carries it away unheard.

"I feel like we've gotten off on the wrong foot somehow. I'm Desdemona," Desdemona takes a hand away from her stomach, reaches across Douglas and extends it through the driver's side window. "And this is my husband Douglas. What's your name, sir?"

The man looks at her hand as if a snake has emerged from her wrist. He puts his right hand to his heart, and nods to her. Desdemona pulls her hand back inside the car. The man inhales and looks at them both like a home appraiser trying to figure out if the structure is worth the investment. He sucks his teeth, and says with his ageless genderless voice, "Round these parts they call me Leg, bruh."

The day now seems to be hurrying toward night. Douglas and Desdemona look from Leg to the ever darkening sky.

"Leg is it? Fantastic. Mr. Leg, please, where is Oscarville Road?" Desdemona asks, unable to mask the urgency in her question.

"All you had to do was ask. Hahaha," Leg throws his head back, laughs to the heavens and begins rocking in his chair. He looks up the road to the right of the tree and says, "Down there you've got Kowaliga Lane. People who've lived around these parts a long time call it

Benson."

Then he points toward the road on the left and says,

"And over there you've got Oscarville Road. There's only one cabin down each. So that must be where you're headed. Just drive until you can't no more, and you're there."

"Thank you Mr. Leg," Desdemona says, her trifecta-sash-winning smile returning.

"Gesundheit," Mr. Leg says to her with a quiet sincerity.

"No one sneezed," Douglas says.

"I never said anyone did," Leg replies, returning them all to the beginning of their exchange.

Leg's words disappear behind a clap of thunder. The wind picks up further, rain clouds begin to gather, and the sun turns fully into moon.

"Hurry now. Storm's coming, almost here," Leg says as his rocking finds the rhythm of the swaying trees. He shows no signs of worry and no effort to seek shelter.

Douglas peers up through the moonroof. "It looks bad, Desi."

"The forecast didn't say anything about rain," Desdemona says as she looks too.

Leg looks past Douglas, at Desdemona, and says,

"It all depends on who's forecasting, but don't worry the worst storms make the best cleansers."

Leg laughs through a wide closed lip smile. He keeps his eyes locked with Desdemona's, and begins whittling and singing again.

5.

There are some roads that appear to be ripped from lore, sketched from classic literature. Roads that you've been told will take you to where you want to go. No matter the promise you still have to traverse them to know where they truly end. Roads that look straight when you're standing at the top of them. That carry twists, turns, and switchbacks that you can't see until you're right up on them. Roads that carry just as many problems as promises. The road to the cabin looks like it's been plagiarized from a Robert Frost poem. In truth it's a road less about where you want to go, and more about where you end up.

Douglas backs up, points the car down Oscarville Road and races the rain, seeing which of them can reach the cabin first. It's clear the rain is going to win. Douglas and Desdemona bounce and jostle down the road-ish path like two kids in a fifty cent amusement park bumper car. Desdemona holds tightly to the passenger side door handle and begins to nervously sing. Music has always been calming to her spirit. Her singing gets louder as she grows more anxious.

"What is that Desi?" Douglas asks, trying to distract them both from the precarious path. The pitch of his voice bounces up and down with the car.

"I don't see anything," she replies as she cranes her neck and tries see what Douglas is seeing. The combination of the now pouring rain and blanketing night reduces her visibility to just a few feet beyond the car's headlights.

"No, what's that you're doing? What are you mouthing?"

Douglas's hands GI-Joe-Kung-Fu-Grip the steering wheel in an effort to keep the car on the path and out of the trees. The dirt road, which is quickly turning into a mud road, causes the car to fishtail on occasion. Desdemona becomes, surprisingly, aware that she's singing, and that her singing is growing in volume.

"Yes, that. What is that?" Douglas asks.

Desdemona continues as if hearing the melody for the first time herself. She's not sure what she's singing initially but then it comes to her.

"Oh! It's what that man, Leg, was singing. I didn't even realize I was singing it."

"Leg, singing?" Douglas says, as the back tires lose and find traction.

"Yes. Yes," Desdemona replies, her eyes wide.

"I don't think anyone has been singing Desi."

"No? You couldn't miss it. Are you serious? You didn't hear him singing? He was rocking, singing and whittling on that..."

Just then they reach the end of the road. The car slides to a stop, and the headlights fall on an A- Frame cedar cabin. A streak of lightning races across the sky making night, for a moment, appear day. In that moment Desdemona sees it. Sitting on the top step of the cabin. A doll with high cheekbones, full lips, hair that though whittled wood looks to be matted wool. The doll's full, round, impossibly white, living eyes seem to stare straight into hers.

The hairs on the back of her neck stand on end, and her hands tent across her stomach.

6.

"He was rocking, singing and whittling on that... doll."

Desdemona finishes the sentence in a whisper. It's not possible. There is no way Leg could have beaten them to the cabin. Maybe it's a replica. Maybe he's whittled a million of these dolls. A roll of thunder cascades and booms like the hooves of the horses swinging low and coming forth to carry us all home. On its heels is another brilliant and blinding bolt of lightning. Douglas and Desdemona duck reflectively. When Desdemona lifts her head and looks back to the porch the doll is gone.

"Did you see that!?" Desdemona shouts pointing to the porch, to the spot where the doll was.

Douglas's head rises slowly and cautiously,

"Yes. Come on."

Douglas begins gathering the few things they have in the backseat.

"Come on!?" Desdemona says, her eyes still focused on where the doll should be.

"Yes! Come on! We've got to get out of this storm. We'll grab our bags in the morning."

With that Douglas opens the driver's side door and sprints toward the cabin, almost slipping and falling on the muddy path along the way. He reaches the porch and keys the access code into the cabin door. He hears the gears of the lock turning and breathes a sigh of relief as the door swings open. He feels a rush of cool air wash over him as it escapes the cabin and dances between the raindrops. He's drenched and tired, but knows he'll be dry and comfortable in a moment. He turns to say as much to Desdemona and only then realizes she's still in the car.

He squints through the storm. She's still in the passenger seat and making no moves to be anywhere else. Douglas waves his arm, gesturing for her to join him. She doesn't. She sits there perfectly still, her legs pulled to her chest. Douglas ducks inside the cabin. He finds the light switch, flips it, and shields his eyes as the front room fills with soft light. He looks around and on a coat rack just to the right of the front door he sees an umbrella. He grabs it and races back out to the car, almost falling again.

He reaches the car, pulls the door handle, and it's locked. He pulls again but still it doesn't budge. He looks through the water streaming down the window, and Desdemona is staring straight ahead at the cabin's porch.

"Desi? Open the door Desi! Come on!"

She slowly shakes her head, no. The rain streams down the window and any part of his body that the umbrella can't cover. He feels his temper rising but knows that anger will get him nowhere. As calmly as he can he says,

"Desi. You can't stay in the car. But if you do then I'm going to have to stand out here all night because I'm not going to just leave you in the car. Please, come out. Come into the cabin, with me. Please."

Desdemona doesn't move. Douglas isn't sure what to do. He's

not sure if anything can be done. Then he hears her whisper.

"I'm scared, Dougie."

Memories of what it feels like to be scared are never far from him. As a bullied boy he lived in, what felt like, a state of constant fear. Fear of being seen, singled out, and known. He eventually turned that fear into anger. An anger he wrestles to control until this day.

Douglas rests his forehead gently against the wet window. He's been running, slipping, and sliding, and the storm has been raging to beat the band. He realizes that never for a moment did he think of how that had to make her feel. One of the things he heard about over and over in their therapy sessions was his need to be more present, more attentive, more thoughtful.

With a voice steeped in concern and wrapped in softness Douglas softly says,

"It's okay. I've got you Desi. I know it's scary but it's okay," and then he whispers, "I know you're scared, but what am I?"

There are a couple of seconds of silence and then the car doors unlock. He grabs the handle and pulls the door open. He pulls Desdemona under the umbrella and they both make the precarious run to the cabin. They cross the threshold, their chests forward like two runners crossing the finish line. Desdemona immediately turns, slams the door closed as if preventing something from running in behind them. She locks it, and sinks to the floor with her back against the door. Her chest is rising and falling like a buoy in turbulent seas.

"You okay?" Douglas asks as he crawls over, water pooling from his clothes with every move, and sits beside Desdemona with his back also against the door.

"You saw it?" she asks.

He assumes her voice is trembling because she's cold. The cabin has been kept cool to combat the summer heat, and with their wet clothes on it feels truly chilly. Douglas jumps up to grab her a towel, and possibly a blanket. Before he can run off she grabs his hand holding him in place.

"You saw it, right?"

He feels the urgency in her grip. He sits back down.

"Yes. That's why I said we had to hurry in."

"That's why you said..." She looks at him, her brow furrowed in confusion and asks, "What did you see?"

"The lightning. It scared me too. It lit up the whole sky."

He realizes she's still holding his hand when she squeezes it so tightly that he winces, and says,

"No Douglas. No! The doll! Did you see the doll!?"

Douglas pulls his hand free, flexes it as if restoring circulation, stands, and sits across from Desdemona.

"The doll? What doll Desi?"

"Are you fucking with me Douglas?" Desdemona moves to her feet but keeps her back against the door.

"Douglas, that man Leg he was singing that song, and whittling a creepy little doll! That doll was sitting out on the porch when we pulled up! And you didn't hear or see any of that!?"

"No Desi. I didn't hear or see..." Douglas reaches for Desdemona. She pulls away, pushing herself further into a door she's already flat against. Douglas takes a step back.

"Desi, I'm not saying... Look, I was just trying to get us here. I wasn't paying attention like that. Plus that dude was weird as fuck. Who the hell names their kid Leg? Is he the left or the right? For balance he better have a sibling named Leg too. I also feel like I need to sneeze twice just to earn all of those damn gesundheits!"

Desdemona's back comes away from the door slightly. Douglas has always been able to disarm her with humor. Even now, through her confusion and worry and in spite of herself, geyser like staccato laughter erupts from deep in her belly. She covers her mouth with her hands in an effort to hold it in, but to no avail. With all of the tension, her body seems to just need a moment of levity and release. Douglas holds his arms out. Desdemona leans forward and steps into his embrace.

"I'll make sure all of the doors and windows are locked, okay. If Chucky or Annabelle or whoever is out there they better not come in here or their ass is firewood!"

"Dougie!" Desdemona says as she wraps her arms around him.

"I'm just kidding. I'm just kidding! In the morning we'll take a look around and see what we can find, and if we see Leg we'll act like we don't. Okay?"

Desdemona moves as close to Douglas as she'd been to the door. He wraps his arms as tightly as he can around her still shivering body.

7.

All things look better and safer in the light of day. The things that go bump in the night always hide away from the day's light. They recede far into the closet, behind the lions and witches in the wardrobe. They disappear deep into the shadows beneath the bed, beneath the dusty throw rugs, and creaking, warped, floorboards. They seem to bide their time and wait for the moon's call.

In the light of the day things that felt terrifying just a few hours ago seem incredibly ordinary and easily explained away. That man you were sure was standing in the corner of your room is nothing more than a coat rack with a hat on it. With the sun on your face that finger from the abyss scratching at the back of your neck is little more than the ever present tag on a shirt's collar. All things look better and safer in the light of the day.

Even if they aren't.

Douglas and Desdemona wake in each other's arms, holding one another with a tenderness they'd misplaced months ago. The events of last night race and rattle around the edges of their thoughts like a car dancing back and forth across a highway rumble strip. Neither of them speak of it. They tip-toe around the subject like the first child to reach the tree on Christmas morning. Douglas and Desdemona ease out of each other's embrace, and roll out of bed in search of coffee.

In the kitchen they discover a kettle, coffee (instant), and a landline phone mounted to the wall. Desdemona picks up the receiver, listens for a dial tone, and hears that age old shrill hum that verifies a phone is indeed in service. She breathes a sigh of relief knowing that with their cells finding no service they at least have a way to reach out to the world. Douglas sees that the phone's number is tacked to the wall just above the phone and types it into his cell's notes app. They both sit, drink their coffee, shower, dress, and walk into a new day.

Once she steps onto the porch Desdemona's eyes immediately go to where she last saw the doll. Nothing. She asks herself, did I imagine it all? Douglas looks at all the downed tree limbs the storm left in its wake. Their car barely escaped the wrath of one. Douglas pops the trunk and takes their suitcases inside.

They decide to head into town, see if they can find some breakfast, a signal for their phones, and run past the bait and tackle shop. They'd planned to link up and go fishing with their friends, but if their cells are down too it might prove impossible to coordinate. One thing at a time though. Right now their stomachs sound like whales sending out mating calls, so breakfast takes precedence.

They jump in the car, pull off, and immediately Douglas realizes that he didn't charge the car last night. The car has more than enough charge to go to town and back, but he'll need to charge it when they get back. The car slides and bounces up the mud covered road they raced down last night. Douglas feels they're lucky that no trees or limbs fell across the road. He reaches across the center console and takes Desdemona's hand. In the distance he sees the top of the great tree. Desdemona squeezes his hand letting him know that she sees it too.

8.

Desdemona releases Douglas's hand and sits forward as they draw near the tree. She's ready to confront Mr. Leg about the doll. She wants Douglas to see it, and hear the song. She wants to prove to him, and herself, that she's not going crazy. The car climbs the tiny hill that the tree lives just beyond. Now they both lean forward with anticipation. They crest the hill. Douglas holds the steering wheel with more force than the moment requires. Desdemona is unwittingly holding her breath. Their eyes simultaneously fall, on an empty rocking chair. They both exhale, look over at each other, and laugh. Douglas playfully wipes his brow like, whew, and slows down. Their eyes search for Mr. Leg like he's a cheetah high in the trees waiting to pounce, but he's not to be found. Douglas loosens his grip, and Desdemona sits back.

They pass the tree and head down Seneca toward the main highway. Desdemona glances at the side view mirror, and sitting, rocking, whittling, and smiling at her is Mr. Leg. He nods to her just as the car bounces violently through a deep pothole in the road. In the car's shaking she loses sight of Mr. Leg. As fast as she can she turns fully around but now the chair sits empty. Rocking but empty.

"Desi, is everything okay?"

"...Yeah."

"You sure?"

"Yeah... Yes."

Desdemona faces forward and softly, under her breath, she begins to sing.

9.

   Desdemona and Douglas pull into the small town. The word small feels right, but town feels like a misnomer. The town, as it is, consists of a dozen poorly paved streets, and a few old weather battered bungalows that surround a town green. The green features a dry fountain with Themis at its center. Themis's hand is extended as an intended water spout, but it looks and feels like a beckoning. Flanking the town square is a bait and tackle shop, a tiny Buc-ee's, an old 24-hour diner offering breakfast anytime, a new-ish restaurant serving lunch and dinner to anyone that meets the dress code, a thrift store, an REI, a grocery store, and a fire/sheriff's station. The town is a dance between high end desires and common folk needs. There are enough wealthy visitors to warrant a new REI, but not enough tax revenues to fix the old roads.

   The day feels freshly hatched, young, and full of promise. The town is abuzz with people up from the city for the weekend flying through the streets. Families, couples, friends, and everyone in-between emerge from REI with new gear, and from the diner with full bellies. The sheer volume of people packing the broken sidewalks would suggest that every cabin on the water has been rented. The boats on the lake are likely to be nestled bow to stern, and the fishing little more than a drunken exercise in getting lures wet.

   Douglas parks across the street from the bait and tackle shop. Douglas and Desdemona step from the car and immediately get swept up in the current of the energy of the day. The movement. The laughter. People walking briskly with somewhere to be. People walking slowly with not a care in the world. After the crazy night they had, they're both happy to breathe deeply, let the sun warm their face, and genuinely smile for the first time since yesterday's sunset. They walk hand in hand across the street and into the bait and tackle shop.

"Desdemona?"

The voice coasts just above a Muzak version of "Achy Breaky Heart" and other country and western hits playing on a loop in the store. Desdemona's eyes scan the shop and fall on Doran. Both of their smiles widen. A familiar face has never felt so welcome. Just as Desdemona is about to point out Doran to Douglas she feels a hand slap against her shoulder and pull her sharply to the left. The next thing she knows she's in a group embrace with Douglas and Doran's husband Wallace who has come up from behind with a stealthy firm hug.

"Of all the bait shops in all the towns in all the world, you walk into this one," Wallace says with a feigned Bogart accent.

"Yeaahhhh seee you dirty rat!" Douglas responds with his best Cagney.

They immediately turn back into college kids. Desdemona escapes the group embrace, bad jokes, and even worse impersonations. She walks over to greet Doran who is smiling and shaking her head.

"They don't ever really grow up do they?" she says as she leans in to give Desdemona a hug and air kisses."No they don't," Desdemona replies as she gives Doran's shoulders a gentle squeeze.

"What can we do? Can't live with 'em, can't throw them in the

198

lake."

"Well, we haven't gotten to the lake yet sooo..."

They both throw their heads back in laughter. Their husbands look over for a second and then go right back into reliving their youth.

"We wanted to call y'all but we have no cell reception up here," Desdemona says, pulling out her phone, holding it aloft, and looking for a signal. She continues,

"It's like we don't even have bars in the places I feel like we had them before."

"Right!" Doran emphatically agrees, fishes her phone out of her purse, and shows Desdemona that she doesn't have a signal either.

"It's crazy. None of the stores have wifi since the storm. They've been going old school. It's either cash or they take an impression of your card with one of those…" Doran starts moving her arm back and forth like she's running a card through a Zip Zap, "you know what I'm saying?"

"Yeah! An old knuckle buster," Desdemona joins her in mimicking the old card running motion. They both laugh again.

"It's so good to see you! Listen, we've got a phone in our cabin. Do you?" Desdemona asks.

"Yes, a landline. Thank God!"

Doran reaches into her purse and pulls out an old receipt that she's written the cabin's phone number on. She rips it in half, re-writes the number, and gives it to Desdemona.

"Here. That's our number."

Desdemona pushes the receipt into her purse and remembers that Douglas has their number in his phone.

"Dammit I don't have ours on me. Douglas has it."
Desdemona turns to go get the number when Doran grabs her shoulder.

"They're having so much fun. Wallace only acts this free and foolish when he's around Doug. Just call when you get back to the cabin and give it to me then."

Doran and Desdemona watch as their husbands become more of who they were and less of what the world demands they be. They smile and Doran begins lightly singing. It takes Desdemona a second to recognize the tune but slowly she realizes it's Leg's song and her smile fades. Faintly she hears another voice join in with Doran, and then another, and another. The singing grows louder. Desdemona soon realizes everyone in the store is smiling, shopping, and singing.

10.

"Doran? Doran! Where did you hear..."

Before Desdemona can finish her question the sounds of screeching tires, a bone crushing crash, and an explosion resound outside of the shop. The windows of the store vibrate and shake as if they're about to free themselves from their frames and explode into a million sharp shards. Instinctively people's heads turtle into their shoulders. All of the singing stops. Everyone looks around as if emerging from a trance. Then, all at once, they rush toward the door. In the frantic wave of movement Desdemona gets knocked to the ground and separated from Doran. She balls herself into the fetal position, her knees hugged to her chest, and covers her head as scared and desperate people step over and on her. She eventually scrambles to her feet and spills out into the street. Her eyes search wildly for Doran, or Douglas, or Wallace. She doesn't see them, anywhere. She looks across the street to their car. Maybe once they got separated Douglas returned to the place he knew she would go. There sitting on the roof of the car, facing her, is Leg's wooden doll. It's wide, white eyes fixed on hers. Asking. Questioning. Accusing. She stares back. Frozen.

"Desi!?"

Desdemona turns and finds Douglas racing toward her. He's running with so much pace he's barely able to stop himself when he reaches her. His eyes are filled with worry and relief.

"Jesus Desi, are you okay? I lost you in the scrum. A car t-boned another and both got pushed into the fountain. One caught fire. Wallace and Doran ran up. I told them I had to find you. I..."

Desdemona can barely make out what Douglas is saying. Her knees buckle and her vision blurs. She's trying to make sense of Doran singing Leg's song and... She slowly turns back to the car. The doll is gone. Again. She sinks to the ground, her hands over her mouth.

"Desi! Desi?" Douglas shouts.

It's the last thing she hears before everything goes black.

11.

In the dark, just past fear, lives comfort and rest. Once the hamster wheel of one's mind stops spinning terror, and the dread in one's heart stops beating fright, there comes a renewing comfort and rest. A sleep so deep that it's been described as death's cousin. Although I'm sure death would demand a DNA test. Beyond angst, is a rest so complete that waking seems an act of cruelty.

Desdemona rouses to the feel of a cool rag across her forehead. It's what her mother used to do when she was ill with fever as a child. She'd wake, wrapped in a comforter, to the smell of tomato soup and a slightly burnt grilled cheese sandwich. The cool, soothing, dampness of a cloth would be laying across her forehead and eyes. She'd eat, tell her mother she felt better, and ask to go outside. Her mother would say, if you're well enough to go outside then you're well enough to go to school. She wouldn't go outside.

Desdemona's mind and body are just beginning to snuggle into that memory when she hears an explosion, sees the wooden doll, and hears Doran singing all at once. Desdemona jumps to her feet so quickly her head swims. She reaches out and grabs the frame of the bed to steady herself. Bed? She looks around and realizes that she's back at the cabin.

"Desi?" Douglas rushes into the room.

Desdemona grabs onto him like he's the only life raft in a turbulent sea.

"It's okay. It's okay," Douglas wraps her in his arms with more warmth than any childhood comforter ever could.

Desdemona buries her head into his chest, feeling herself on the verge of tears but not entirely knowing why.

"What happened to me?"

"You passed out. You turned toward the car and collapsed. Wallace had just come back from trying to help the people in the crash. He checked you over and said you were probably overheated. That I should bring you back to the cabin and..."

"Did you see it?"

Douglas looks into Desdemona's eyes and sees the same look of fear and confusion he saw last night.

"... Desi, come on now."

"So that's a no?"

"No. All I saw was you in distress."

"I swear to you. I swear to you! It was there! It was there last night and it was there today."

"The doll?"

"Yes! The doll! And Doran was singing that song. Leg's song. Everyone was singing it. There's no way you didn't hear that!"

"I didn't hear it. Not from Doran, not from anyone."

"Am I going crazy!?"

Desdemona sits down on the bed, her full weight falling like an anchor to the ocean's floor. She looks out of the bedroom window and stares at the full moon, high in the dark sky, making night look like noon.

"What time is it Dougie? How long was I out?"

"It's late. You were down for hours."

"We need to go to Wallace and Doran's right now!"

"Desi, slow down. You're just coming around after passing out, plus it's late. Wallace told me they're in the cabin down Kowa… whatever. Down the road on the other side of the tree. But we don't even know if they're still up."

"Doran gave me their number. It's on a receipt in my purse. Where's my purse?"

"Still in the car I think."

"Please. Please get it. Call them. Please."

"Okay, Desi. Okay. Wait here. Please, try to calm down."

"Okay. Okay. Please get the number."

Douglas eases out of the room as Desdemona pulls her knees into her chest and hugs them. She begins to slowly rock back and forth just as the door closes. Douglas stands, his forehead against the bedroom door. The sound of the squeaking bed springs as Desdemona rocks seems to echo, hauntingly, through the cabin. Douglas takes a deep breath, turns, and walks out of the front door into the night.

12.

    In the darkness of night things that looked and felt incredibly ordinary just a few hours ago can seem terrifying. That pile of dirty clothes in the corner of the room can suddenly appear to be breathing and moving. The tapping on the other side of your bedroom window, that you were sure was a tree branch a few hours ago, now sounds like an incessant invitation to a dark and eternal destination. You know it's all in your mind, though.

    You hope it's all in your mind.

    Perhaps it's because of the change in temperature or it could be a result of Desdemona's constant talk of unseen wooden dolls and unheard songs, but something shoots a shiver down Douglas's spine as he slowly moves toward the car. He steps gingerly, like he's negotiating a minefield, but he has no idea what he's tiptoeing around. He doesn't realize his hands are shaking until he reaches for the car's door handle.

    He opens the door. The dome light doesn't automatically come on. He disabled that setting when he bought the car. Tonight he wishes he hadn't. He looks around in the dark for the purse, and anything that might go bump in the night. His eyes fully adjust and he sees it, the purse, sitting on the backseat, unmoving and benign. He begins to reach for it but stops, his hand hovering, loathe to touch it. He feels like it will grab him if he tries to grab it. He steels his nerves, juts his hand forward, taps the purse and quickly pulls his hand back. The bag wobbles a bit from the touch. Douglas lets out a nervous laugh, shakes his head at his own irrational fear, and grabs the bag.

Instead of heading back inside Douglas sits in the car with the purse in his lap. He feels like he needs to calm down and center himself before going back into the cabin. He and Desdemona can't both be on edge. He takes a few deep breaths, turns on the dome light, and goes through the purse looking for the phone number. It doesn't take long to find the torn receipt, or to discover that she has more gum and lip gloss than the law should allow. He puts the receipt in his pocket, turns off the light, and runs back to the cabin like hellhounds are on his heels.

13.

Douglas walks, winded, to the bedroom and finds Desdemona standing, looking out of the window. In the window's reflection he can see that her mouth is moving, but there's no sound.

"Desi?"

Desdemona continues to stare into the night, at the moon, at the stars. It's the same blind stare Leg had when they first encountered him. Her mouth moves passionately and soundlessly. The veins in her neck swell, her hands ball into tight fists, and Douglas can tell that she is saying, or singing, something with everything that's in her.

"Desi! Desi!?"

Desdemona turns to him, her silent song now pushing her mouth into a distended hyena's grin. Her jaw bounces up and down, extended beyond reason and possibility, like a Pez dispenser come to life. Her fists begin to violently beat a rhythm against her thigh as she begins to slowly walk toward Douglas. Tears stream down her face, as her eyes frantically search the room as if looking for a way out. Douglas wants to run to Desdemona and wrap her in comfort and safety, but his feet betray him. His feet moving steadily away, back through the bedroom door. Desdemona rises up on the balls of her feet. The tears clear and her eyes flare just before she charges. Douglas is able to slam the door shut just before she reaches him. The second the door closes he feels her fists beating a violent and desperate rhythm, with all her might, against the cedar. The hinges shake and the jamb creaks but the door holds. He spots a small chair, in the hall, just across from the bedroom. He sits on the floor, keeping his back against the buckling door, extends his leg and hooks the chair with his foot. He pulls the chair to him, wedges it between the doorknob and floor, then rushes into the kitchen and grabs the phone.

Douglas pulls the torn receipt from his pocket and dials the numbers. He can hear Desdemona down the hall pounding against the door. He doesn't know how much more the door can take. The other end of the line starts ringing. Douglas juggles the receiver but catches it before it falls to the floor. He presses the phone to his ear.

"Pick up. Pick up! Pick up!!"

He repeats the words over and over like a mantra, like a prayer, to anyone and anything that is listening. The phone rings and rings and rings, and then suddenly his prayer is answered. Someone on the other end picks up the receiver.

"Wallace! Wally! Hello? Hello! Doran?"

On the other end there is no reply.

"Doran! Doran!?"

Douglas pushes the phone as close to his ear as he can and then he hears it, a beating, a drumming. The same drumming, the same rhythm, that's coming from down the hall is coming from the phone.

14.

Douglas slams the receiver down and runs toward the front door. He stops, turns, and runs back to the bedroom. He puts his hands against the door and can feel it shaking. He shouts through the Cedar,

"Desi! I don't know what's going on! I don't know, but something is happening! I'm going to run over to Wallace and Doran's cabin! I'll be right back! Stay here! Please stay in the room! I love you! I'll be right back! I love you!"

Douglas sprints to the car and heads up the road at breakneck speed. He rounds the tree and slams on the brakes skidding to a stop. Illuminated by his headlights, sitting in a chair in the middle of the road, rocking, is Mr. Leg.

15.

Douglas lays on the horn. Leg just rocks and smiles with his head tilted forward and down. Douglas backs up, hits the gas, and charges forward, the tires spinning and kicking up gravel. The headlights bring Leg closer, and dangerously closer, until finally Douglas stomps the breaks. The car skids to a stop again, inches from the rocking chair.

"Get out of the fucking road!" Douglas shouts.

"Get out of the fucking car." Leg replies his voice even.

Douglas is out of the car and racing toward Leg as if he's still in it. The thought of his wife going through a mental breakdown back in the cabin, and this man barring the way forward, only adds pace to his strides. Douglas feels his breaths coming in and out, short and choppy, like he's hyperventilating. He draws a fist back intent on knocking Leg out of the chair, and wiping that smile off his face before dragging him out of the road. He's seven paces from Leg. Six. Five. Four.

"You can't hear the song can you?" Leg says, his head still tilted forward and down.

Two paces from Leg, his fist trembling with anger, Douglas stops, frozen in place. His chest heaves up and down and through short choppy breaths and gritted teeth he says,

"My wife keeps saying she's hearing some song. A song she heard you singing. I thought she was going crazy. I haven't heard any song. But you... you can hear the song?"

"Me? No, I can't hear it. I know it."

"What? What does that even mean!?"

"That means that I can't hear it either. It was taught to me as I slept beneath that tree," Leg points to the tree at the crossroads roughly ten yards away, "by the children of the lake that used to be land."

"The children of the..."

"The lake that used to be land. You know Lake Siri wasn't always here."

"Leg..."

"That Lake. Lake Siri, it's a man-made lake."

"Leg, please move, I have to..."

"A hundred and fifty years back there was a thriving Black town, right there. Right where the lake is. Freed Black people took the low land that no one wanted and planted roots. Grew a community. At its peak there were over a thousand Black folk, happy, working, and making plenty money, right there. More money than the people in the White town, on the high ground. You were probably over there early buying breakfast, or bait, or some bullshit."

"Yeah. I was in town but...."

"But one day a White man said that a White woman said that a Black man or boy did or said something to her. Well that's all it took. There was a dam that kept the river from flooding into the low ground. The White townsmen went and knocked it down. In an instant more water than can be drunk flooded the low ground drowning damn near the whole town. The townsmen's rifles and nooses took care of anyone that didn't submit to a watery grave. That was a hundred and fifty years ago, tomorrow. Well, shit, it's midnight so I guess that was a hundred and fifty years ago, today. That's how Lake Siri was made. A tide of genocide."

"What does that have to do with, anything?"

Leg, whose head has been slightly bowed, looks up into Douglas's eyes, and with a distended hyena's smile he begins to sing a song dark and consuming. A song that lives somewhere between a psalm of redemption and a dirge to get you to the other side. A song that makes all who hear it want to run, and dance, and pray, at the same time. A song that neither of them can hear.

"All round the hills and streets of dark towns

for days and weeks in dark towns

the mobs gathered to say, Obey Obey,

or we'll give you gills in Dark towns.

Write out your wills now dark towns

Poseidon take hold your heels now dark towns

the mobs gathered to say, Away away

Dam they soon drowned the Dark Towns."

Leg stops singing, and his mouth seems to bend back into something humanlike. Leg stares into Douglas's eyes, clears his throat and says, "You didn't hear a word did you?"

"No."

"Me neither, but you could see I was singing couldn't you?"

"...Yes. What the fuck is going on!?"

"You seen Benson Stone? Your wife probably describes Benson Stone as a doll about yay tall."

Leg holds his hands roughly a foot apart.

"No! But she keeps saying that she keeps seeing some..."

"Some, what?"

Leg sits forward. The car's headlights illuminate the fullness of his face. Douglas opens his mouth as if to continue, takes a look at Leg, takes a deep breath, and stops himself.

"The words come hard before me? Go on, I won't be offended!"

Leg lifts his head high, his dark skin all but glowing in the headlights. The beams make the edges of his nappy hair look aflame. Like the burning bush that told Moses to take off his shoes. Leg's smile showcases all of his perfect, white, wolf's teeth.

"Go on and say it!"

Leg waits but Douglas doesn't fill the space. So Leg says it for him, "She keeps seeing a pickaninny curio. That's what they're called in museums. A nigger child doll. That's what they're called in thrift stores and yard sales. But around these parts, by those who know better, they're called Benson Stone."

"They?"

"Yes, they. They are the children of the lake that used to be land.

214

They taught me the song. They are carved from wood in the image of heaven and have been known to drag people to the depths of hell. And you, YOU can't hear the song, or see Benson Stone?"

Leg waits again. Again Douglas doesn't fill the space. This time Leg isn't going to do the work for him. Finally Douglas erupts.

"No. No! I've already told you, No!"

Leg pulls a thin piece of plant root from his front breast pocket and starts chewing on it. He regards Douglas for a second, squints and says, "You really don't know do you?"

Douglas shifts his weight nervously from foot to foot like a kid in the principal's office after being told their parents have been called.

"… What? I don't know what?"

Leg's jaw drops and the chewing stick falls to the ground. With equal parts surprise and realization he shouts, "Oh shit! You DO know don't ya! HAHAHA!"

Leg throws his head to the sky, and rocks back in the chair. His laughter seems to bounce off of the trees and carry to the moon.

"Know what!?" Douglas shouts.

"Only White folk can see Benson Stone, and hear the song! "

Douglas balls his fists again, and squares his shoulder.

"I don't believe in any of this bullshit, Leg! Now get the fuck out of the road!"

Leg raises his hands in mock surrender, stands, moves the chair out of the road, and continues speaking as Douglas sprints back to the car.

"Only White people. I can't hear the song. I just know it. That unlucky bastard the sheriff's got locked up for no reason he can't hear it. And you, YOU can't hear the song."

Douglas opens the car door, turns, and shouts back to Leg who is now sitting by the side of the road and rocking in his chair.

"Fuck you and your accusations!"

"They call me Leg Bruh! I've been sitting at this crossroad since God decided to play Build-A-Bear. Don't try to pull Leg. You know who and what you are, but thing is you pretend too long, believe too hard, and you'll mess around and become what you ain't. HAHAHA. There's one last verse! The lost verse! Let me sing it for you!"

Leg can feel the deep breaths coming in and out of his lungs, his diaphragm contracting, and his throat burning with effort. He knows his mouth is opening wide and closing like a Venus flytrap. He's aware that he's singing, and continues to do so as Douglas drives off.

"A hand rose from the graves of Dark Towns

Up through the waves of Dark Towns

A hand that waved this way, this way

Join us now down in Dark Towns."

Speeding away, in the rear view mirror, beneath the light of the moon, Douglas can see Leg. His mouth has distended into a clownish smile. His jaw seems unhinged, and his fists are beating a violent rhythm against the arms of the chair.

16.

Suddenly up ahead there is an intense and fast approaching light. Douglas pulls his eyes from the rear view mirror and puts them on the road. A car with its high beams on is in the middle of the road and racing toward him. Douglas, sure that he is in a losing battle of chicken, pulls the steering wheel hard right. The car shoots past him. Douglas's car fishtails into a spin. He thinks, do you turn into the spin? Against the spin? Before he can come to a definite answer he slams into a tree. The airbags deploy, keeping him from slamming his head into the steering wheel, but a full-on impact with an airbag is no day at the park either.

Douglas stumbles out of the car, dazed, but fairly sure that the car that almost hit him was a lake blue Levin electric. Wallace and Doran's car. Shakily Douglas begins to walk and slowly jog back up the road. He reaches the crossroad where Leg now sits. Douglas ignores him and turns to run down the road to the cabin, to Desdemona.

"No use going down there," Leg shouts, "they already went down there and picked her up."

Douglas stops in his tracks, and bends at the waist with his hands on his knees. He hasn't exerted himself like this since college.

"What!?" Douglas says while sucking in as much air as he can. He continues when has enough oxygen in his lungs to say more than one word. "Where'd they take her!"?

"I didn't ask and they didn't say but they came back up the road something urgent, and turned off down there as if heading toward the lake. Truth be told, road looked to be full of people headed to the lake tonight. Odd time for a swim. All of them looked to be singing, but I couldn't hear a thing."

"How do I get there, Leg!?"

"Well there's the road of course, but if you're on foot, which you seem to be, you can cut through the woods. Just follow the moon, she's full tonight. She'll lead you there sure enough."

Douglas wills his feet to move. His first couple of steps are unsteady but he soon finds his stride. His legs and lungs are on fire, but he pushes through the pain. Low hanging branches slap across his face and sharp briars pull at his pants as if trying to keep him from the lake, but he won't be denied.

He pushes past the woods and onto the lake's shore. The lake is filled with boats. Fatigue forces him to stop and catch his breath. Douglas looks over at the boats and sees that bow to stern, port to starboard, every boat is filled with people standing against the far railings. They all appear to be singing to the lake. Douglas looks at the water, he sees nothing, but the people on the boats see—floating in the lake—hundreds of curios. Hundreds of Benson Stones. One for every person on the boats.

Douglas spots them. Desdemona, Wallace, and Doran are standing, staring at the water, and singing, on a boat about thirty yards off shore. Douglas can't know, but they've reached the final, lost, verse and in unison they all sing

"A hand rose from the graves of Dark Towns

Up through the waves of Dark Towns

A hand that waved this way, this way

Join us now down in Dark Towns."

With the last word, all at once, all of the curios sink beneath the water. The unheard voices of the people on the boats echo over the lake. Douglas sees that everyone's mouth has stopped moving. In the air is a stillness that feels complete.

Through the calm he calls out, "Desi! Desi!!"

Desdemona looks up and over toward the voice calling her name. She sees Douglas, and their eyes lock. She smiles, and winks at him, just before she steps off the edge of the boat and sinks beneath the water along with everyone else.

Douglas shouts. Adrenaline gives his muscles a strength that rejects exhaustion, and he races to the water. Douglas dives in. He swims to the boat Desdemona jumped from, and submerges into the dark, cold water in search of her. He stays beneath until his lungs cry for air and a moment longer still. He surfaces and dives again and again. There is no Desdemona, no anything, no anyone. There is just a lake full of empty boats, the full moon, and the distant echo of a song he can't hear.

17.

The first police car stops by the lake around ten the next morning. The officer finds Douglas sitting by the shore, his knees pulled into his chest, rocking. The officer says a relative of one of the boaters, unable to reach her, called and asked for a wellness check. He notes the eerie silence, empty boats, and asks Douglas where everyone is. Douglas replies matter-of-factly, and in little more than a whisper.

"Dead."

By the afternoon news cameras, police, friends, and relatives are everywhere. The authorities drag the lake, and send in divers, but no one is found. The lake is full of empty boats and surrounded by abandoned cars. The cabins are filled with personal belongings. It's clear that the people were here, but where are the people now?

That's the question asked over and over of Douglas when he's taken to the local fire/police station. He tells the police about the man at the crossroads, Leg. They go there and only find an empty chair. Douglas tells them about Desi, the song she said she could hear, all of the people on the boats, and their apparent mass suicide. He tells them that he swam out immediately and didn't find anyone. They ask him the same questions in different ways but his story never changes. Finally they have no choice but to release him.

They give him the requisite paperwork he needs to process out. Standard questions. Name, address, age, and race. Douglas holds his pen hovering inches above the, Black or African American, box on the form. He looks around the station at the White men in uniforms and then toward the back, where the cells are, and he sees a lone occupant in a lonely cell. Some unlucky Black bastard. Even in a town so small as to not even be a town, the inescapable imbalance of things seems to hold true. Douglas sits up straight, clears his throat, and checks White or Caucasian.

The police tell him not to leave the state, and that they'll contact him if they have any more questions or if any new information emerges. He thanks them. He gets in his car, and plugs in his cell phone. The phone comes to life and a digital voice intones, "*GPS Signal Found.*" Douglas starts laughing and dissolves into tears. He grabs a tissue from the glove box to wipe his eyes, pulls down the visor mirror, and sees that he's begun to sing. His mouth is distended and his jaw impossibly extended. Douglas doesn't recognize the person in the mirror. He reaches up and touches his face to ensure it's actually his own reflection. It is. He clasps his hand over his mouth, uses both hands in an effort to force his jaw together, but he can't seem to make himself stop singing. He doesn't know the song. But he can hear it. He's hearing it for the first time as he's singing it. The song feels old in his soul. It moves at a pace reminiscent of gospel or blues. There's a darkness to it. A consuming darkness. He wants to run, and dance, and pray. He doesn't know how but already knows the words. Douglas looks over at the passenger seat and sitting there is a small, one foot tall, childlike figurine carved from distressed walnut; with high cheekbones, full lips, hair that though whittled wood looks like matted wool, and full, round, piercing, living eyes. Impossibly white eyes. Benson Stone.

# *Bolie*

[Inspired by The Big Tall Wish
by Rod Serling || Fiction]

# *Bolie*

## [Inspired by The Big Tall Wish by Rod Serling || Fiction]

"... Maybe there is magic. Maybe there's wishes too. I guess the trouble is... I guess the trouble is, there's not enough people around to believe. Good night boy."

Those were the last words Bolie spoke to me before I fell asleep on a warm spring night twenty years ago. I was an eight year old boy looking for a hero and Bolie was a thirty-eight-year-old man looking for a second chance, a bus to glory. Earlier that evening Bolie found himself center ring at St. Nick's Arena in a ten rounder against up-and-coming boxer Joey Consiglio. Bolie was giving away ten pounds and fifteen years to Consiglio. The odds were against him. The crowd was against him. Hell even Thomas, his own corner man, had bet against him. But I believed in Bolie. I believed beyond belief. And if he could do it, if he could take a tiger by the tail and pull off an upset that no one saw coming, it just might put his life back on track. He might be able to hold his head high when he walked down Lenox Ave. He might be able to hold a conversation without his eyes finding his feet. He might be able to hold my mother's hand, a hand he stared at more than anything else in this world, and ask for it in marriage. Bolie was fighting for more than a championship belt and a winner's purse. He was fighting for respect, for a chance, for his life.

Though thirty-eight, Bolie looked much older. His face was a map and journal of his defeats. Sometimes, after school, he'd take me to ball games and on walks. He'd speak glowingly about the wins early in his career, but inevitably his face would darken and his voice would take a melancholy tone as he grumbled about the cuts he'd gotten across his forehead fighting in St. Louis. His speech would slow to a crawl as he recalled how he'd gotten his nose broken twice in the ring in Syracuse. His fingers would softly run over keloids on his cheeks as memories of a tough opponent, and the poorly done stitches he got after a fight in Miami, came flooding back. Bolie was older than most fighters, heavier than he should have been, and almost blind in one eye but still the ring called to him like a Siren's song. In the ring he knew he still had a puncher's chance. He could still land that devastating right that would send his opponent to the canvas unable to stand for ten seconds and find Bolie once again holding a championship belt, once again on that bus to glory.

My father had been the stuff of fairy tales. The stuff of myth. The stuff of bedtime stories. He'd been little more than an amusing piece of folklore people would share with me from time to time that didn't seem to be based in truth. My mom said he was around until I was about two, but I don't remember him at all. Not his face, not his touch, not his voice. There was an old shirt in my mom's closet that she said was his. Proof of a life I suppose. She said it still smelled like him. It always smelled of cigarettes and mothballs to me. It always smelled like smoke and poison.

Bolie must have moved into the apartment upstairs when I was three or so. He was at the beginning of the end of his boxing career even then. When I was small and we'd go for our walks, people would stop him on the street and talk about his past victories. *Bolie Jackson! Man, I remember that night in Madison Square Garden when you...* or, *Bolie! My guy! I won a hundred dollars when you beat so-and-so at such-and-such arena.* He stood tall and proud. As he lost more and more he was stopped less and less. His back, straight, began to bend a bit. His shoulders, square, began to round. His head, held high, began to bow. He no longer saw himself as the man he had been, my mom seemed to always see him as the man he could be, and in my eyes he was the definition of what a man ought to aspire to.

Then came the evening of April the 8th, 1956. Twenty years ago. The fateful night when Bolie stepped into the ring against Consiglio. He and I both knew it was his last chance. His last grab at the tiger's tail. Bolie needed something stronger than a good right that night. Bolie needed magic. Not the stuff that makes a card appear from a deck but the stuff that stops time, bends reality, and changes lives. I was sitting on my mom's knee watching the fight on DuMont TV, and early on I could tell something was wrong. Bolie wasn't using his right, his most powerful weapon, at all. Consiglio was all over Bolie like cheap suits on local politicians. How Bolie survived the first three rounds was a miracle, but in the fourth an uppercut from Consiglio sent him down. He was down and not getting up. I jumped from my mom's knee, pressed my face against the TV, and I made the big tall wish.

What is a wish if not a prayer. What is a prayer if not asking a higher power to intercede. What is that intercession if not magic. Bolie needed prayer. I wished for intercession. What happened was magic.

Bolie went from on his back, and being counted out, to on his feet with Consiglio unconscious on the canvas. The count was *7...8...9...10, You're out!* The referee waved his hand to signal the fight was over and raised Bolie's high above his head. The belt and winner's purse were his. My mother and I jumped up and down with excitement. We must have woken half of Harlem! The half that wasn't already watching the fight that is. There I was with full knowledge of the miracle, of the magic, that had just happened. My mom and the world were none the wiser.

Bolie came home excited and confused. I was on the roof feeding the pigeons in their coops, thinking about the magic of flight, and still glowing from Bolie's victory. Bolie came over all smiles and "How'd I look!?" I told him he looked like a real champ. He said that he couldn't remember winning. That, in truth, he remembered losing, but then suddenly his hand was being raised and he was being carried out of the ring on people's shoulders. His eyes searched mine for answers, and that's when I told him. I felt I had to. I told him that I'd made the big tall wish. That I'd made it for him. I told him that the moment wanted, no needed, magic. There was no other way. No other path to victory, to success, to respectability. But Bolie couldn't accept it. He couldn't believe. Life had proven to be all hard fists and deep cuts. It had shown itself to be concrete and steel beams, rope burns and red lines. A world like that doesn't have room for miracles, for intercession, for magic. And since he couldn't believe, it couldn't be true. Not for him. Not for me. So in an instant, it wasn't.

I woke up in my bed after the fight to find Bolie sitting there. His right hand was wrapped. The map and journal of his face replete with new roads and chapters. His win turned into a loss. I lay there eight years old, and even today, doubting that the magic had ever happened. Doubting that magic was real. I told Bolie that night, "I ain't gone make no more wishes Bolie. I'm too old for wishes. And there ain't no such thing as magic, is there?"

Bolie replied hesitantly, "I guess not Henry." Then added, "Maybe there is magic. Maybe there's wishes too. I guess the trouble is... I guess the trouble is, there's not enough people around to believe. Good night boy."

I went to sleep that night and when I woke, almost as if with the wave of a wand, Bolie was gone. Mom said he moved out in the middle of the night. He needed the purse from the fight to make rent. After losing, instead of facing the landlord, he disappeared. I ran up to his apartment. The door was open. The place was cleared out. The only thing left was a pair of boxing gloves. The one's he'd worn the night before. Right there, right then, alone in that empty flat holding a pair of worn boxing gloves, Henry Temple the boy, Henry Temple the believer, vanished.

Soon after, mom lost her job, and around August of '56 we ended up moving with family down south. Macon, Georgia. Just a year earlier Emmett Till, a boy just a few years older than I was then, was killed, murdered, lynched in Mississippi. The late 50s, down south, were an eye opener. Lynchings, hoses, and dogs. Backdoors and Whites only water fountains. It was a tough time and a tough place to be brown, alive, and trying to make a living. Mom eventually got a job as a domestic and a waitress. I helped as much as a young boy could but the stress and physical demands soon found her in bad health. By 1962, around the time of Billy Randall's Macon bus boycott, she was completely bedridden. I dropped out of school at fourteen to work and help support her. I was young but the men that needed their peanut, peach, and pecan crops harvested didn't care about age, just productivity. I was productive.

I was fifteen when Dr. King stood on Lincoln's steps in Washington D.C. and started speaking of dreams. This was also around the same time that some friends and I, children, were attacked at Tattnall Square Park by a group of grown White men just because we were Black and happy where we allegedly weren't supposed to be. They rained fists and bats down on us until their arms grew tired and our bodies grew still. Tattnall Square was where the map and journal of my face began. We were told that if we returned something far worse would happen. The stabbing of Louis Wynn a few days later proved the veracity of their statement.

In that same year, 1963, Medgar Evers and JFK would be killed. Two huge steps backward in the fight for justice and equal rights. In 1964, the Civil Rights Act would be passed. A step forward. In 1965, Malcolm X would be assassinated. A step back. In 1968, Dr. King and RFK would be assassinated. Two more steps back. The steps forward didn't seem to be keeping pace with the steps back. Then in 1970, after years of battling her failing health, my mother passed away. Her death didn't make the paper. It's not written about in the annals of history or the chronicles of time, but there was no greater step back for me personally. I was twenty-two and felt as old and alone as any one person could. For the next few years I lived in a deep and abiding fog. Days blended into nights, and months into years almost without me noticing. By the time the fog lifted, and I was able to register time and space once again, it was 1976 and I was driving a city bus for the Macon Transit Authority. I knew my route by heart but couldn't tell you how long I'd been working there or how I'd even gotten the job. I just knew that this was what I did and this was how I did it.

All of this brings us to today, an unremarkable Thursday in April of '76. I'm driving my route as usual. My route comes with few changes or surprises. It's one of the reasons I like the job and route so much. My life has been too malleable up to this point, and I need something, anything, that will hold its shape. At the first two stops no one gets on. This isn't unheard of, but rare. The empty bus gives me a few extra moments to breathe easily. Some time to think my own thoughts. It's 9:30 in the a.m. as I begin to pull away from the 3rd stop, the bus still empty. That's when I look into the side mirror and notice someone running after the bus waving their arms frantically. It's an old man laboring with each step. My foot hovers between the gas and the brake. I don't have to stop. I've actually been told by the MTA not to stop. Company policy is that once you've passed a bus stop, continue lest you throw off the route's timing. I'm enjoying the empty bus to be honest, and would certainly enjoy it for another stop or two, but I always stop for people running a little behind. In a world that offers few breaks, especially to Black folk, it's the small acts of kindness that blow wind in your sails and keep you going. A driver stopping for me if I was running late is what I would want, so it's what I do for others. I hit the brakes, open the door, and a winded man boards. He steps on panting and through a mouth gasping greedily for fresh air he says, "I finally did it. I finally caught a tiger." He lifts his head and his face is a map and journal that I know so well it could be my own. Cuts suffered in St. Louis, a nose broken twice in Syracuse, keloids created in Miami. Through watering eyes, a furrowed brow, and trembling lips I say, "Bolie?"

I turn the bus off and stare into the face of a man that disappeared the second I told him magic was real. I open my mouth to speak and before I can Bolie says, "I couldn't face you Henry. I couldn't face you or your mother. I know everyone thought I left because I couldn't make rent, but if I'd have run every time I couldn't make rent I'd have been an Olympic track hopeful instead of a boxer."

Bolie laughs at his joke. I do not. I'm not entirely sure I'm not having a stroke or suffering the effects of an aneurysm. Something is making me hallucinate because Bolie being here isn't possible.

As if reading my thoughts Bolie continues, "It's really me Henry. It's really me!"

Bolie grabs me by the shoulders and pulls me in for an embrace. My body is an immovable object. My strength and resolve are that of a man, not a boy. A man that doesn't want to be hugged. Bolie's ever-present smile fades.

He gives my shoulders a soft squeeze, lowers his head, and in a voice that is almost a whisper says, "I ran from you and from myself Henry, but what they say is true, no matter where you go there you are. I

231

bounced from place to place. Literally. I was a bouncer at clubs in Newark, New Rochelle, Hartford, and parts in-between. Each town came with new cuts and scars but nothing cut deeper than knowing I'd won." Bolie lifts his voice and his head. His smile returns like the sun peeking through gray clouds after a hard rain. I see in his eyes that he's clearly reliving the moment, that night, twenty years ago. "I remember winning, Henry! Standing in the middle of the ring, a winner. Every night, no matter where I was, when I closed my eyes and went to sleep I could feel my hand being raised in victory. Every day, no matter what I did, my heart knew. My heart knew I was given the ultimate gift but I was too scared, scarred, and hurt to receive it. Whenever I looked at the sky I could see the loving faces of you and your mother when I came home that night. When I got dressed to go to work, to go anywhere, I could feel the pats on the back from the people on Lenox when I walked from St Nick's to Harlem belt in hand." Then, once again, the sun of his smile fades as another dark cloud, another dark memory, drifts in. "I also remember telling you that there was no such thing as magic. That there weren't enough people who believed." Tears well up in his eyes and begin to fall just as his smile re-emerges as wide as I've ever seen it. Down south when the sun shines while it's raining people say, the devil's beating his wife. Bolie's face is a living breathing representation of that joy and pain. "Then I did it Henry. I made the big tall wish. I wished I could tell you face-to-face how sorry I was. How sorry I am. I wished with everything in me and the next thing I knew I was an old man chasing a bus and, for once, I caught it. I caught you. I caught a tiger! Henry, I'm sorry. I'm so very very sorry."

Bolie stares at me, and I finally find my voice, "How are you here Bolie?"

"I... I just told you Henry. Magic."

"Bolie, there's no such thing as magic."

"No, no no no. Don't say that. There is Henry! There was then and there is now. There's real magic in the world Henry, you just have to believe."

"Mom's dead Bolie."

"I, I didn't know Henry."

"How could you know? She died in a bed that wasn't her own, in unbelievable pain. Where was magic then? Do you know how many times I've been called a nigger. How many cuts and scars I have from White fists, and broken bottles, and police deputized dogs? Where was magic then Bolie!?"

"Henry..."

"No Bolie! There ain't no magic. There wasn't any then. There isn't any now. So please, get off my bus." I look at my watch and it's 9:40, "I'm already ten minutes behind on my route and I can't afford to lose the one thing I know I can believe in. A check."

"Henry you've got to believe or it won't be true! You know that better than anyone! You've got to believe Henry."

"If magic is true then you wasted it Bolie because I don't believe. I don't believe in magic... and I don't believe in you. I don't believe!

Now, get off my bus!"

My teeth bare. I look down at my watch as my hands tightly grip the steering wheel, and it reads 9:30. I look up, to insist once again Bolie leave, and he's gone. I look behind me and find an empty bus. I look in the side mirror and there is no one running late. No arms waving. No old man struggling. I shake my head to clear out whatever cobwebs and illusions have found their way in there. For the rest of the route I find myself looking at, staring into, intently searching the side mirror at each stop.

I barely speak another word for the rest of the day. People board and say good morning, or how are you this afternoon? All I can manage is a nod of my head in acknowledgement. When I park the bus at the depot at the end of my work day my boss sees my face as I exit and asks if I'm okay.

"You look like you've seen a ghost, Henry."

He receives the same head nod everyone else has. It's the only response I can muster. I ride home on a bus just like the one I've driven all day. I enter my second story walk up and begin warming last night's beans, which will also serve as tonight's beans. The silence I've maintained continues, but still I hear Bolie's voice. Every word. His face and words are the sum total of what I remember from today. Today. I look at the calendar. April the 8th, 1976. Twenty years to the day. I begin laughing and crying. The devil's beating his wife. I fall across my bed. The laughter comes to me so hard that my stomach begins to cramp and the tears flow into my ears.

"I wish you'd have believed me that night! I wish you'd have believed me that night Bolie!!"

"Henry. Henry?"

I look up and find my mother standing in my bedroom door.

"Henry what are you yelling about?"

I jump out of bed before I know what I'm doing. As I do I catch my reflection in the bureau mirror. The bureau mirror in my bedroom, in Harlem. I stop and stare at eight-year-old Henry Temple. He stares back, his face a blank slate. His face a map with no roads. A journal with no entries. This is the face of Henry Temple the believer. I touch my own skin as if it's a long lost and missed friend.

"Henry? Baby? You okay? You look like you've seen a ghost."

With tears that usually only accompany the most severe spankings I run to my mother, wrap my arms around her waist, bury my face into her stomach and shout, "I love you!" between body-wracking sobs.

"I love you too honey! What's going on!?" My mom pries my arms from around her waist, takes my face in her hands and says, "Are those boys at school picking on you again?"

I laugh, say no, and hug her again. I embrace her in the hopes that my hugs will keep her here. Keep her with me. Keep her alive.

"Henry, I don't know what's gotten into you tonight, but there's someone here to see you," and with those words Bolie steps into the bedroom holding the championship belt.

"Hey! What do you say Henry Temple! How'd I look tonight?"

"Like a winner, Bolie. You looked like a real winner."

# *Rose Colored Glasses*

[a Short Screenplay]

# Rose Colored Glasses
## [a Short Screenplay]


CHARACTERS:

JOHN TETLEY (FATHER)

JANE TETLEY (DAUGHTER)


INT. OUTSIDE OF BEDROOM DOOR.


>JANE TETLEY hears the voice of JOHN TETLEY in
>conversation coming from the other side of his bedroom door.


>JOHN TETLEY

>No Margaret! HAHAHA No! I said no, and I mean it!

>HAHAHA!


Jane opens the door, enters, and looks around. John sits
in a chair looking just to the left of the television. He's wearing
his favorite, red-tinted, shades. Jane turns off the television.


>JANE TETLEY

Dad? You talking to the TV again?

JOHN TETLEY

I ain't never talked to no TV. I didn't even know the damn

thing was on.

JANE TETLEY

You don't remember turning it on?

JOHN TETLEY

I remember you turning it on because you were tired

of talking to me.

JANE TETLEY

Noooo.

JOHN TETLEY

Yessss.

JANE TETLEY

Who were you talking to then dad?

239

JOHN TETLEY

... Nobody.


JANE TETLEY

You were in here having a full on belly laugh with

nobody?


JOHN TETLEY

I was talking to... You know what, never mind. I already

know what you think. You think I'm crazy.


JANE TETLEY

No one thinks you're crazy dad. It's just...


Jane picks up a prescription bottle sitting beside a full glass of

water next to the television.


JANE TETLEY

Listen, have you been taking your Donepezil?

JOHN TETLEY

Hell naw!


JANE TETLEY

Dad. There's no cure for, the A word.


JOHN TETLEY

The A word? Being an asshole? Are you calling me

an asshole?


John and Jane both laugh.


JANE TETLEY

No Dad! You know what I'm saying.


JOHN TETLEY

I don't know what you're saying until you say it.

So say it.


JANE TETLEY

Alzheimer's. Are you happy? There is no cure for

Alzheimer's yet, but the doctor said the pills will help

until they find one, AND that they're getting close. Okay.


JOHN TETLEY

Well, I truly pray they find that cure, and the people with

old timers...


JANE TETLEY

Alzheimer's.


JOHN TETLEY

Whatever it's called. I hope they get the help they need.

I don't need no Dope-pez, no Deep-pends, no Dumb-pres,

no none of whatever it's called!


JANE TETLEY

Donepezil.


JOHN TETLEY

Well, whatever! If anything, before your mom passed,

I just needed a little Viagra. But that's about it.

JANE TETLEY

Ewww dad!


JOHN TETLEY

Before the little blue pill it was like trying to play pool
with a piece of rope!


JANE TETLEY

Dad, stop!


John laughs. Jane opens the prescription bottle and takes a pill
out. She picks up the glass of water and extends them both to
John. John turns his head. She sits them on the stand beside him.


JANE TETLEY

Dad, will you take off those shades. I want to see
your eyes.


John doesn't comply. Jane lovingly lifts the shades to the top of his head. John looks lost. He squints and looks around the room as if desperately searching for something or someone.


JOHN TETLEY

Margaret? Margaret. It's Scoop! Your Scoop. Margaret!?


Jane places her hand on John's in an effort to calm him.


JANE TETLEY

Please take your medicine. I miss mom too. I wish I could see her again too but she's gone. Please, stay with me dad. I can't lose you too.


John picks up the pill, puts it in his mouth, and drinks the water.


JOHN TETLEY

Your mother's not gone. She's always been here. Will always be here. I will be too. Janey, some things you have to see to believe. And some things you have to believe to see.

John pulls the shades back down. He looks to his left, just beyond his daughter, smiles and nods.

INT. HALL. A FEW DAYS LATER.

John is walking to the bathroom when he overhears Jane on the phone.

JANE TETLEY

Yes. No, he's getting worse. More and more he thinks he's talking to my mom, and sometimes my grandparents. Yes, I've been giving him the pills you prescribed. I don't think they're working. I don't know if I can... I might have to put him in care.

John goes quietly back to his room.

INT. HALL. OUTSIDE OF JOHN'S BEDROOM DOOR. LATER THAT DAY.

John sits in his chair wearing his shades. Jane stands with her ear to his bedroom door. She listens as he speaks passionately.

JOHN TETLEY

She thinks I'm crazy! She's going to put me away! I won't allow it Margaret! No, dad don't make excuses for her! I didn't work all those years at the AJC and put her through college just so she could put me away. No!

Jane opens the door, rushes in, and looks around the room.

JANE TETLEY

Who are you talking to dad!? The TV's not even on so you can't make that excuse.

JOHN TETLEY

I've never made that excuse! That's your excuse so you won't think I'm crazy. Which I'm not!

JANE TETLEY

Dad. I can't.

JOHN TETLEY

I know, you can't do this. I know, you might have to get me, "Care."


JANE TETLEY

Have you been listening to my conversations!?


JOHN TETLEY

Have you been listening to mine!?


John starts looking around the room and shouting.


JOHN TETLEY

No ma, I will not! Dad! Margaret! Margaret don't you dare take her side! Don't you dare!


JANE TETLEY

Dad? Dad, easy. I'm sorry. Calm down, please.


John stands up from his chair. He begins pointing around the room.

JOHN TETLEY

You don't! You don't! Tell ... me...


John collapses onto the floor. His shades fall off. Jane rushes

to his side.


JANE TETLEY

Dad!


With trembling hands John reaches for his shades.


JOHN TETLEY

Margaret! Dad! Ma!


JANE TETLEY

I'm here dad! I'm here! I'm calling an ambulance!


Jane pulls out her cell phone and dials 911. John's hand

reaches the shades.


JOHN TETLEY

Janey. My Janey. I love you.


JANE TETLEY

I love you too dad. Hold on, help is coming.


John extends his shades to Jane.


JOHN TETLEY

These are for you.


John drops the shades before he can give them to Jane.

His hand and body go limp. He closes his eyes.


JANE TETLEY

Dad? Dad! Dad!?

Fade to black.


INT. JOHN'S BEDROOM.


Jane enters John's bedroom dressed in black. She's just returned

home from his funeral. She sits in his chair and tearfully looks around his room. She sees his favorite, red-tinted, sunglasses sitting on the nightstand beside his chair. She wipes her eyes and puts the sunglasses on in an effort to feel close to him again. She gasps and quickly removes them. She slowly pulls them back on. She looks around the room and smiles.

JANE TETLEY

Pop Pop? Nana? Mom?

Jane breaks into tears.

JANE TETLEY

Hey, dad.

# *Prestidigitation*
## [a Short Screenplay]

# *Prestidigitation*
[a Short Screenplay]

CHARACTERS:

LANCE WINNINGTON (FATHER | MAGICIAN)

LAURIE WINNINGTON (DAUGHTER | NANNY)

MARK AND CINDY DUMAS (LAURIE'S EMPLOYERS | UNSEEN)

NEWS REPORTER (VOICEOVER)


APRIL 5TH, 1968

INT. HOUSE - DAY


LAURIE stands in the door of the home she shares

with her father and waves goodbye to the husband

of the family she nannies for, MARK. Mark has driven

Laurie home after she's worked a shift, overnight, watching

his newborn baby. Laurie is still wearing her apron with

a pair of salad tongs tucked in the tie string.


LAURIE

Thank you for the ride Mr. Dumas! Yes sir! Absolutely!
Please tell Mrs. Dumas not to worry, the fresh diapers are
in the closet, the bottles are in the Frigidaire and I'll be
back later this evening. Yes sir. Drive safely.

Laurie closes the door and rests her back against it.

LAURIE

Lord have mercy! First time parents! They thinks every
rash is smallpox and every poop a parade. You'd think
that baby was crapping out James Brown records or
something!

Laurie mockingly sings.

LAURIE

Say it Loud! I poop and I'm proud!

Laurie laughs loudly and then notices that the house seems
empty.

LAURIE

Dad? Dad you here!?

There is no response. Laurie looks around the house but LANCE, her father, is nowhere to be found. She looks in the kitchen and sees a broken drinking glass and the back door ajar.

LAURIE

Dad! Dad answer me!

Laurie looks out of the backdoor at the room above the garage. There's a light no. She runs up the steps and bursts into the room.

INT. GARAGE -DAY

Laurie finds Lance in the middle of the room with his sleeves rolled up and both his hands inside of a top hat. He's visibly straining with great effort. The hat sits on a table covered by a cloth. He doesn't acknowledge Laurie's entrance.

LAURIE

Dad! Did you hear me calling you?


Lance doesn't respond.

LAURIE

Dad?



LANCE

Yes. Yes I heard you.


Laurie sits, takes off her shoes, and starts rubbing her feet.


LAURIE

Well, why didn't you answer me then?



LANCE

... Because I was busy.



LAURIE

Busy doing what? Busy breaking glasses and not closing

the back door? Busy worrying me? Busy about to get us

robbed, again? Busy up here in your magician's lair pretending to pull a rabbit out of that hat?

LANCE

I'm not pretending.

LAURIE

What do you mean you're not pretending? Did you forget that I know all of your magician's secrets? I know how you do all your tricks, dad. There's a false bottom, and a trap door, and a rabbit under the table cloth.

Laurie walks over and lifts the table cloth. There's no rabbit.

LAURIE

Where's the rabbit?

LANCE

There is no rabbit. I'm not trying to do a trick. I'm trying to pull a rabbit out of this hat, for real. I'm trying to do, I need to do, real magic.

LAURIE

See! That's why Mark and Cindy don't have a TV. It makes you go crazy. Fills your head with madness. What have you been watching, Bewitched? I Dream of Jeanie?


LANCE

The News.


LAURIE

The News? Well I ain't seen no news. I was tending to Mark and Cindy's newborn all night. And if the news is what's making you think you can pull Bugs Bunny out of a third hand hat, I don't want to watch it, and I don't want you to watch it.


LANCE

How are the dumb-asses?


Laurie sighs.

LAURIE

... Dumas. It's Mark and Cindy Dumas.


LANCE

That's not how we pronounce it.


LAURIE

Who is we!? You and Harvey the damn rabbit?


LANCE

Me and anybody with any sense. I told you, you don't
have to work for no White folk. You don't have to scrub
floors, and burp babies, and warm beds.


LAURIE

Wait a minute now! Ain't nobody warming no beds!


LANCE

Well you ain't got to do none of it.

LAURIE

Did you hit the number and forget to tell me?


LANCE

No.


LAURIE

No? Well then I have to keep on doing what I'm doing.

Which again, does not involve any bed warming. You

know good and well that we can't make it on the little

bit of money you're making in those run down, chitlin'

circuit, juke joints, playing pick a card any card.


LANCE

We made it this far.


LAURIE

Did WE?


Lance takes his hands out of the hat.

LANCE

What's that supposed to mean?


LAURIE

Nothing. I'm tired. Please, drop it.


LANCE

Oh, it means something. What's it supposed to mean?


LAURIE

...Why do you think mom left?


LANCE

I see. You think it was because of me.


Laurie sucks her teeth.


LAURIE

I think she was tired of struggling, dad. I think she needed

a man with both feet on the ground, instead of his head in

the clouds. I think she needed hard cash.

260

Laurie pulls out the salad tongs tucked in her apron, waves them in the air, walks over to the table and taps the hat.


LAURIE

And not fuzzy bunnies pulled out of hats.


Laurie holds out her empty hands and sits back down.


LANCE

Well your mother had her own kind of magic.


LAURIE

Well, I guess it's my turn to ask. What's that supposed to mean?


LANCE

Nothing. I'm tired. Please, drop it.


LAURIE

Stop it, dad. After she left you never talked about it or her.

So, what happened?

LANCE

… You're not a little girl anymore.

LAURIE

Correct. So tell me.

Laurie continues rubbing her aching feet.

LANCE

Your mother had the kind of magic that could turn a
husband into a husband and a boyfriend across town.
And a then one boyfriend into two. The next thing I
knew, abracadabra, she disappeared into the night. And,
zim-zala-bim, so did all the money in our joint savings
account. Then voila I was a single father, with no money,
raising a daughter.

Laurie stops rubbing and moves to stand. Lance extends his hand

and gestures for her to sit.

LAURIE

Dad I...

LANCE

Didn't know? I tell you what else you didn't now. You

didn't know how many meals I pulled out of thin air.

You didn't know how many ways I made out of no way.

You didn't know how many times I pulled rent out of my

ass. You think it's all parlor tricks and bullshit but I

promise you, I'm the most magical motherfucker you

know!

LAURIE

I'm... Dad I'm, sorry.

Lance wipes his eyes, walks back to the table and puts both hands

back into the hat. Laurie walks over to Lance.

LAURIE

I didn't mean to... It's been a long night. I'm really and

truly sorry.

Lance doesn't respond. Laurie looks at him, and then at the hat.


LAURIE

Please stop. Dad please. Stop! What are you doing!


LANCE

I told you! I'm trying to pull a rabbit out of this hat! I'm ...

I'm trying to prove there is real magic in the world. There

has to be. Especially today. There has to be.


LAURIE

Why today!?

LANCE

When you walked in I knew you didn't know. I knew the

dumb-asses had you hold up in that house with no tv and

no radio, and so I knew you didn't know.


LAURIE

Didn't know what?

Lance nods toward an old transistor radio sitting by the far wall.

Laurie slowly walks over, picks up the radio, and turns it on.


NEWS REPORTER

... mourners are still gathering in front of the Lorraine
Hotel here in Memphis, Tennessee. The air is filled with
the sound of sorrowful wails as reality continues to crash
down upon them and the world. Last night at 7:05 p.m.
Dr. Martin Luther King Jr. was pronounced dead at St.
Joseph's Hospital...


Laurie screams and drops the radio, breaking it. The broadcast
stops.


LAURIE

What? No. No no no! NO!!!!


Lance continues focusing and straining with both hands
inside the hat. Laurie runs over and tries to pull his hands
out of the hat.

LAURIE

Stop it! Stop it, dad! What are you doing!?


Lance pushes her away.


LANCE

I told you! I'M TRYING TO PULL A RABBIT

OUT OF THIS HAT!


Lance knocks the hat off the table, sinks to the floor, and begins

to cry.


LANCE

If I can do it. If I can pull a rabbit out of that hat. If there
is real magic in the world, then maybe I can save him.
Maybe I can put the bullet back in the gun. Maybe I can
make your mother come home. Maybe I can make you
stop hating me and love me again. Maybe.


Laurie begins crying and sits down on the floor beside Lance. She

takes his hands into hers.

LAURIE

Dr. King. Dr. King is gone, dad. And mom, she's not
coming back. But I have never not loved you. I'm sorry if
I ever made you doubt that. You don't need magic for my
love. It's right here.


Laurie takes the tongs out of apron, swirls them in the air and taps
herself on top of her head.


LAURIE

Tah-dah.


Through tears Laurie and Lance hug each other tightly.


LAURIE

Come on, let's go down to the house before someone
robs us for real.


They both laugh, and help each other stand. Lance turns
and takes Laurie's face gently into his hands.

LANCE

I need you to know two things.


LAURIE

Okay.


LANCE

I love you.


LAURIE

I love you too.


LANCE

And you owe me a radio.


LAURIE

You gone have to start warming some beds if you want

a new radio.


They laugh, exit the garage, and close the door.

A rabbit emerges from the hat.

# *The King Stays on the Board*

## [a Novel || First Chapter]

# The King Stays on the Board
## [a Novel || First Chapter]

My phone buzzes on the nightstand like a nest of federally indicted murder hornets, waking me from my sleep. The phone lights up like my father's face after his third drink; a single malt Scotch that came in a clean glass with a dirty look. I mirror that dirty look as I roll over in bed toward the buzzing light. My hand stops-and-frisks the nightstand, knocking a half read copy of *Dark Green* and a half full glass of water onto the carpet. I finally grab the phone, and squint into the bright screen. My vision adjusts and the caller's name appears. Adam Ryan. The man with two first names. The man that always has to have the last word. Adam from Brooklyn. My boss.

I look at the time. 2 a.m. This can't be good. I've never received a call at two in the morning that was good news. The last call I can clearly remember receiving at this hour was from my mom. She'd called to say that my father had taken his last third drink. The cancer that lived in his liver had metastasized, and grown hot and hungry. Have you ever seen a lone burnt chimney, and nothing else, standing where a house used to be? The ground charred black. The surrounding grass covered in the soot of yesterday's joy. The lot, once a picture of promise, of hope, of what is, now defined by loss, by grief, by what was. The burnt chimney being the sole survivor of a fire that raged so hot, that only the one thing built to withstand such heat was left to mark where a home once stood. Where a family used to live. When the fire of cancer rages and burns through the body the only thing built to withstand that kind of heat are the bones. That's all my father was when he passed. Bones. They stood as a marker of where a life once was, where a man used to be.

One week after that 2 a.m. call, my eyes heavy with tears that refused to fall like stubborn leaves on fall trees, we buried the burnt chimney, the bones that cancer had picked clean and left behind. Then something I hadn't expected happened. My father's presence grew in my mind and spirit. I found myself talking to him more as an ancestor than I ever did as my living breathing father, and oddly I found that he responded more too. Calls at two in the morning still feel, to me, like sickness, like dying, like death is waiting on the other end of the line. Is Adam calling to tell me he's sick, dying, or dead? That would be welcomed news. I know, I know, I'm not supposed to say that. So I don't. I just think it.

Verna is beside me, knocked out, snoring. Something she swears she doesn't do. I keep trying to get proof but it's like her snore is a sentient being that can sense any form of recording device. The second I hit record on anything, her breathing turns into the sound of an angelic puppy sleeping peacefully in a noise canceling cloud. The second I hit stop it's like a tree is being sawed in half, inside of a starved polar bear's stomach. Not that the color of the bear is important. All bears matter. Did I mention that this race-less imaginary bear is also driving a car with no muffler, and probably has no license or registration? But that's beside the point.

I slide silently and gently out of the bed, careful not to wake her. I have no idea why. Remember that small earthquake that hit Atlanta last June in the middle of the night? She doesn't either. My right foot finds the carpet, and the half spilled glass of water that has soaked into it. Me and my soggy right sock ease our way into the living room and settle down on the couch. Verna and I found this couch tattered and torn at a yard sale. Some people rescue dogs, we rescued a couch that kind of smelled like a dog. In my mind I was convinced that the large, intimidating, heavily tattooed, Russian gentleman that had a weekly yard sale of rotating furniture, was selling off the possessions of the people he'd murdered the week prior. Possible homicide aside, he did have amazing bargains. We both immediately fell in love with this couch. It had character and was well built so we Fabreezed it, and then refurbished it ourselves with the help of copious Youtube videos. I settle down on the poorly refurbished couch, take a deep breath, and answer the phone.

"Hello?" I say in my, no-I-wasn't-sleeping-comfortably-beside-an-unmufflered-chainsaw-raceless-bear, voice.

"Joseph!?" comes the response.

I never understand why people dial your number and when you answer, ask if it's you. Instead of, who the fuck else would it be answering my phone at this hour, I say,

"Yes."

"Joseph, it's that time of the month."

To the casual listener you might imagine that my boss has an extensive, intimate, and inappropriate knowledge of my wife's menstrual cycle. Extensive, intimate, and inappropriate knowledge that he shouldn't have. To the casual listener you might think that I should be jumping, via wifi, through the phone and strangling this man for his brash impertinence. Well, number one, my wifi is not the best. Number two, he isn't talking about the inner workings of my wife but rather the inner workings of my job.

I work as an accountant for The SETI Group, one of the largest equipment finance corporations in North America. I took the gig as a temporary position. A placeholder until I saved enough money to chase my dreams. That was six years ago. My dreams are still running, but I've stopped chasing. You know how it goes. I went from freelancing and riding the bus, to a steady check, a decent car, and a decent place to live. Then I met a decent woman, and we had a decent time dating. A decent engagement ring, and a decent wedding soon followed. That's when the snoring began.

Adam from Brooklyn and I started temping for SETI on the same day. From day one everything with him was a competition. He asked me how tall I was during our new hire orientation. I said, six feet. As I looked down at him he made direct eye contact with me and said he was six one. I cocked my head to the side like a confused cocker spaniel, which in retrospect is what I think our couch originally smelled like. From that day forward I avoided looking at him, because my mother told me to never look crazy in the eye. I decided not to dwell on the bold impossibility of his statement, lest I have a stroke.

Adam also has a penchant for using words that he clearly does not know the meaning of. One day after arriving late to work he told me that he'd been pulled over by the police. He said he was only going five miles over the speed limit and couldn't believe he was being ticketed. He informed me that he was completely "elated" with the cop. I said, "You were happy about the ticket?" He said, "No, I was pissed! I was so elated I could have killed the guy!" I just stood completely still and hoped maybe, like a T-Rex, his recognition of presence was attached to his sight, and if I was still enough, maybe, just maybe, he wouldn't be able to see me. Turns out, he could.

To his credit though Adam is a wizard with numbers, and once told me that he never imagined that he would be doing anything other than what he's doing now. He said as a child with an unusually weak bladder he kept a detailed accounting of the number of times he'd wet the bed. Two hundred and forty three. Did I mention that he's also an over-sharer?

Senior accountant and beyond, at The SETI Group or some other major corporation, has been his life's only aspiration. So, early on, while I was treading water and trying to find a tributary to my dream, Adam was swimming his way to the top and drowning whomever he needed to along the way in urine. I looked up one day and he was my boss. A fact that he was sure to let me, and everyone else, know. When other people asked me how I felt about Adam's promotion I told them I was, "elated."

Adam is tonight, or this morning depending how you tell time, on my phone reminding me that it's End-of-Month. That's what, *it's that time of the month*, means at the job. End-of-Month for accountants is always a -- racially ambiguous -- bear. It's reports and reconciliations. It's spreadsheets and ledgers. It's about making the numbers tell inconvenient truths for some and convenient lies for others. Why Adam is calling me at two in the morning to say it's End-of-Month is beyond me.

Instead of saying, get off my phone you definition deficient dumb ass, I say,

"True, it is End-of-Month."

"... if that's true then why don't I have the close of month spreadsheets?" he says.

"What?" I respond, "I sent them over earlier tonight, around nine."

I grab my laptop to check my email and verify that I did in fact send the close of month spreadsheets over around nine. Shit. The laptop is dead and the cord is in my nice car in our nice parking space. Almost on cue my phone starts beeping, letting me know that it doesn't have much charge left either. Keeping the various devices in my life charged is indeed a ministry to which I do not belong. I tip toe into the bedroom and grab Verna's phone, which has more charge than mine but is also almost dead. What a pair we make. I log into my email on her phone and there it is, the close of month spreadsheets. Unsent. Did I mention that my internet is not the best?

"I apologize Adam, it looks like it didn't go through."

"You apologize. You apologize? Accounting is a detail oriented job Joseph. My years at SETI have shown me..."

I tune him out. I want to remind him that we have the exact same number of years at SETI. I'm sure however that just like he looks up to tell me he's taller than I am, he'll look down from his position and tell me he's been at SETI longer than I have. Then I hear it. A word that doesn't belong.

"So, just so that you know Joseph, you not sending the reports when you were supposed to behooves me."

Behooves? Be-fucking-hooves!? Maybe he means befuddles. Perhaps bemuses. But he definitely does not mean behooves! Before I can stop it my inner Inigo Montoya whispers,

"I do not think that means what you think it means."

"What?"

"What, what?"

"What did you say?"

"Never get involved in a land war in Asia?"

"... What!?"

"Nothing. Listen, I'll be sending the report right over. Goodnight Adam."

"Joseph if I don't have that report in the next ten minutes..."

"I know, you'll be elated. Good night."

I hang my phone up just as it dies, and make a mental note to take off this soggy sock and put both phones on the charger before I go back to bed.

Using Verna's phone I make sure the spreadsheets are still attached to the email and resend it. I wait to be sure the email goes through. I need to verify that it moves from the unsent to the sent folder. It does. I set the phone down and breathe a sigh of relief. The last thing I need is Adam emailing me bac... Before I can finish that thought the phone buzzes. Well, that was fast. Whatever mistake he's found must be on the first line of the first spreadsheet. And if the first line is off, the whole first spreadsheet is off. And if the first spreadsheet is off, they may all be off. Shit, I may have to re-do the whole thing. This may be the kind of night that turns into day.

I look at the phone and it's a text message, not an email reply. A text? Adam doesn't have this number. I used Verna's phone but my work email. Before I can think better of it, I open the text.

*You're probably sleep and I hope this doesn't wake you but I just had to say that I miss you, and ache until I see you again. 'Night. - Bee*

I don't know what this is but suddenly I feel like a fire, a cancer, is just starting to rage and wrap itself around the bones of my marriage.

# Acknowledgements

Barbara Starkey Goode. John E Goode Jr. Tiffany Goode. Joshua Goode. Cheryl Goode. Leisa Goode. Duane Goode. Yvette Goode. Big Cuz Cellus. Tracy Ingraham. Dr. Fahamu Pecou. Dr. Lia Bascomb. Dr. Rhea Combs. Faith Carmichael. Janice Barton. Sanjay Patel. Gunther Gordon. Spinxx. Tamika Brown. Ebony Stewart. Lynnette Johnson. The Arman Family. E Rouse. E Bryant. George Dawes Green. Erika Patoni. Jayme Alilaw. Ariana Francesca. Adan Bean. Kerly and AP. Christine Platt. Katina Pappas-DeLuca. NEXT Atlanta. Art Farm at Serenbe. Atlanta Bushwick Bookclub. The Red Cabin. Woodruff Park Chess. New Haven Library Basement Chess. The Village Market. Dr. Key Hallmon. The Moth. Black Coffee Atlanta. Jamin and Ayron. Grant Park Coffeehouse. Portrait Coffee. Ebrik. WABE. MARTA. Soccer in the Streets/Station Soccer. SCAD. 100 Miles. Deva Newman. Chelsea Riddick-Most. Cola Rum. Amir Sulaiman. Q-Swon. Bonnie Harvey. Dana Gilmore. Renita Walls. Malik Salaam. Rekeela Hawthorne. Shane Sleighter. Malik Moody. Verta Maloney. TaJuana "T-Bone" Clayton. Vicki Brown. Richmond, Virginia. Oak Grove/Bellemeade/Blackwell. Atlanta Georgia. St Simons Island. Yin Yang Cafe. MooreEpics. Bennie Morris. LeMor. Atlanta Checkmate Club. Atlanta's storytelling community. Atlanta's spoken word community. Coffee. Pizza.

# *Luther Vandross*

[The King Stays on the Board ||
More True Than Not]

# Luther Vandross
## [The King Stays on the Board || More True Than Not]

Luther Vandross stood in the middle of Woodruff Park laughing beneath a flickering yellow streetlight and a blood moon the color of convenience store bottom shelf rosé. Spasms of laughter caused him to double over at the waist as if cramping in one moment, and throw his head back with his mouth wide open as if a dentist had told him to say, ahhhh, the next. Standing with his head reclined and mouth agape, the strobe from the streetlight bounced off his gold grill and danced through the park with the magic and sparkle of the Studio 54 disco ball on its last night. Luther was surrounded by a group of men sharing in the laughter, and finding joy in their shared circumstance. A circumstance that most wouldn't find humorous, joyous, or common.

The night's humidity—that many evenings served as his pillow, his comforter, and his bed—draped the men like a second skin. A second skin that was feeling no pain as they drank deep into the night. Someone, somehow, from somewhere, had "stumbled" across a small cache of Deep Eddy Ruby Red Vodka mini bottles. Like pebbles on a rocky beach the empties, the dead soldiers, littered the ground and were trampled underfoot. Drunken laughter ensued and rang out into the night. Luther looked at this gathering of men that had been dealt a bad hand that they refused to fold. Each of them Sisyphus with their feet set and their hands firmly against the boulder. Each of them Prometheus in chains watching the eagle as it swoops down for the butcher's meal. He felt oddly proud to stand amongst them. To be a part of this community of the discarded and forgotten.

Just then a voice said, "Fuck you Luther Vandross! I'm mad at you bruh!"

To be clear he's not *that* Luther Vandross. He is instead a man that shares the name, but none of the fame, and certainly none of the fortune. A man whose mother was conceived in the back of a Cadillac Eldorado to the sounds of Luther Vandross's debut album, *Never Too Much*. A man that was himself, seventeen years later, conceived in the back of a Regal to the smooth sounds of a newly released Luther Vandross's greatest hits album.

His mother had seen men walk in and out of her mother's life. She herself had been picked up and put back down again and again like a bad penny. The only man that ever stayed, whose voice she heard through the good times and bad times, who whispered lullabies of love in her ear as she fell asleep, was the R&B balladeer Luther Vandross. So at the age of eighteen when she had her first son she thought, what better name? Her hope was that he'd be more than she, and her mother, and her mother's mother, had found men to be.

Your parents can want great things for you but it's still incumbent upon you to achieve greatness. You can be named Luther Vandross, Julius Caesar, or even Jesus Christ but it's up to you to live up to the name; and that's considering that you even have a desire to sing a song, defeat a Gallic tribe, or walk on water.

This Luther Vandross wasn't big, "So Amazing," Luther

Vandross. He wasn't even little, "Reflections," Luther Vandross. He wasn't the type to stick and stay. He wasn't the kind to sing of eternal love softly in your ear. It's not that he didn't want to live up to the name, he just didn't know how to. He too had heard the songs, but he'd never actually seen this *so amazing love* the ballads swore existed.

For his own life, Luther got into trouble early and often. He was derailed and never seemed able to get back on track. Bad decisions, that felt necessary, put his freedom in the hands of judges. Judges that never gave people as brown as Luther slaps on the wrist. They always threw the book. A book he'd never learned to read.

The bad breaks left him and his mother with a relationship that couldn't be mended. The last time he was locked up she told him that upon his release he'd need to find somewhere else to stay. He walked out of Fulton County Jail and straight to a bench in Woodruff Park. The park has been home ever since.

The voice shouted again, "Luther Vandross! Fuck you!"

The vodka-fueled laughter continued to echo through the park as Luther, and three or four of the dozen or so men in the park that night, turned to face the source of the exclamation. It was Red, or as he was better known, Dirty Funky Red. Luther looked at the seething anger in Red's face and erupted into a chortle that caused everyone else to laugh all the more.

"It's not funny Luther Vandross!" Red said, his feet digging into the ground and his eyes beginning to burn with angry tears.

Luther wiped laughter's tears from his eyes, cleared his throat, and said, "I apologize, Red. I didn't realize I..." he stifled a laugh trying to bubble to the surface and continued, "I didn't realize I was even laughing."

Red took a deep breath. His stance softened, but his eyes remained stinging and skeptical. Luther walked over and put his hand softly on Red's shoulder.

"Now tell me, what is your dirty, funky ass mad at me about!?"

With that, again, the entire park broke into raucous laughter. Red pushed Luther's hand off his shoulder.

"You know what I'm mad about!"

"I promise you Red, I don't."

"Last week you beat me up Luther Vandross!"

"That's not true Red! I didn't beat you up. I just knocked you out."

The men hanging in the park all agreed that Red hadn't been beaten up, just knocked out. The distinction being that Luther hit Red once and Red lost consciousness, but once unconscious Luther didn't continue to beat or stomp Red. Which is something most people in the park would have done. Thus Red was knocked out and not beaten up. The distinction didn't matter to Red.

"I don't fucking care! I'm still fucking mad at you!"

Red's words now seemed to carry within them a hint of danger, and a clear desire for revenge. Luther, who had been caught in the laughter and joy of the night, suddenly sobered. He was no stranger to the sound and feel of threat, of danger, of an enemy emerging. He snorted a deep breath of the thick air deeply into his lung, looked Red in his eyes, and said, "Listen Red, that ass whipping was driving down the road minding its own business. You decided for no reason at all to step in front of that ass whipping."

Red opened his mouth to speak but before he could Luther lifted his hand to signal that he wasn't done. He then walked forward until he and Red were almost nose to nose.

"I feel it important to tell you now Red, that there is another ass whipping riding down that same street. I advise you strongly to stay your ass on the curb this time."

Between the two men there was only air, opportunity and a tense silence. The moment felt like an eternity as it passed. Then one of the drunken bystanders shouted, "God damn Luther Vandross that was some poetic shit," and everyone again broke into laughter.

Luther took a step back, reached into his pocket, pulled out two unopened mini bottles of Vodka, and handed them to Red. This was as much of an apology as one could hope to receive in Woodruff Park. Red nodded to Luther as an acknowledgment of the gesture, and took the bottles. Red opened one of the bottles and Luther opened one of his. Both men drank while staring at each other angrily, and then both men burst into laughter.

"Fuck you Luther Vandross!" Red shouted, his voice playful and light.

"Fuck you Dirty Funky Red!" Luther bellowed back his voice devoid of menace.

Luther and Red laughed and drank with the rest of the men in the park until the small bottles ran out.

In the morning the empty containers, and men, lay scattered across the ground. Luther woke, the sun hurting his eyes, and took inventory of his community. He smiled at this group of kings that, no matter what, stay on the board.

www.ingramcontent.com/pod-product-compliance
Lightning Source LLC
Chambersburg PA
CBHW020543020726
47494CB00006B/1890